NEXUS

A.J. Winters

A special thanks to my wife for creating such a beautiful cover as well as a special thanks to Cheeto and RampantStrawberry on Penana for following this story to its end.

CONTENTS

1/VOICES

James peered over the ledge he was perched on. Cold mountain air caressed his cheeks and sent a shiver down his spine. Goosebumps broke out across his skin. This was a place he went to when feeling lost, as somehow the raw beauty of nature always pulled him out of a funk.

Standing a thousand feet off the ground, he could really soak in the raw beauty of the forest below. Pine trees peeked out of the fog as it rolled through the valley, coating the grass with crystal clear dew. Deer could be seen grazing, leaping through the marshes and grassy fields as a lone eagle flew overhead, letting out a piercing screech.

Despite the majesty of the scene, James couldn't feel happy, not anymore. He found it impossible to feel anything at this point in life. No happiness, no sadness, no hate, and no love – even the fear of falling was no longer present as he inched closer to the edge. *I have — am — nothing.*

He wasn't always like this. When he was young, his heart was sensitive, maybe too sensitive. But that changed as the world around him devolved into a crime-infested sinkhole. The cries for help from the innocent victims of this rotten world pierced his brain and wouldn't go away. It angered him that bad things happened, but it angered him even more that he couldn't do anything to stop it.

In this world, you were either born a superhero or a nobody, and he was a nobody. His brother wasn't a nobody; his brother was one of the highest-ranking superheroes in the world. He had it all: looks, power, money, fame. That was exactly the problem. The heroes of the world didn't act like heroes anymore. They were just idols and glorified celebrities. They used to stop crimes and save the innocent, but now they just soaked up adoration and money from the less fortunate. James knew that if he stepped off the ledge, there would be no one to save him, not anymore. He had no intention of actually jumping. He merely wanted to force an epiphany, trick his mind into sending one last jolt of emotion, any emotion, flooding into his heart.

Before he moved further, a faint voice called out to him, begging him to step back. A strange sensation accompanied the whispers – a desire to flee, to run away. The urge became stronger the more he fought it, eventually winning out. For now, James decided it would be best to just go home.

He got back to his apartment and jingled through his keyring while trying to find the one that opened the door. The keys dropped to the floor, causing him to turn around to pick them back up, which forced him to face the door across from him. That apartment belonged to an older, yet lively lady named

Mary. He liked having her as a neighbor. She was quiet and very kind. Anytime she baked, she would always offer him a plate of cookies, muffins, or whatever it was she decided to make. He would always help her carry her groceries upstairs when she got back from the store, and he enjoyed doing it for her.

"At least I can be a hero for you, Mary," he mumbled into the musty-smelling hallway.

After jiggling the key in the lock, the door swung open. He threw his clothes onto the floor of his bedroom, adding them to the growing piles that peppered the carpet and took a long, hot shower. Dinner was a frozen serving of chicken fingers and mashed potatoes reheated in the oven – his standard go-to. He watched TV until bedtime just like he did every day, either that or playing video games. With his lonely routine complete, he brushed his teeth and slid under the covers of his unmade bed. The sweet release he would gain from not having to be awake lured him into a quick, deep sleep. Finally, he could escape reality for a little while before starting the entire pointless day all over again.

The only problem was James found it impossible to shut his eyes. He couldn't get comfortable as he rolled around in his bedsheets, now made damp by sweat. It felt like there was a massive weight on his body, causing his heart to pound and his chest to tingle. Opening his eyes, he looked over at the alarm clock. It read 2:45 a.m. in a bright red hue.

He tried ignoring the feeling of unease, but it

only grew. He was about to get up and get a glass of water, but when he tried to move, he found he was locked in place. His arms and legs had become frozen and refused to respond to his commands.

He didn't panic. This was not the first time he experienced sleep paralysis. His calm soon turned to fear when standing in his room not five feet away, he noticed a dark figure.

James squinted in the darkness to determine if he was really seeing what he thought he was. All doubt vanished as the shadowy being crept closer to the bed. James tried to get his body to move, but all attempts to escape failed. It was now right next to him, and his eyes were wide with fear. The figure looked down at one of his exposed feet peeking through the covers and reached its hand out towards it. Instead of grabbing James' foot and dragging him out of bed, the being just took hold of his blanket and covered his exposed foot. James went from horrified to puzzled.

"Nice little place you got here." The creature spoke in a calm and soothing tone. The statement was a flat lie. Between the month-old food lying atop the dressers, and the carpet of unwashed clothes no sane person could make such a comment in good conscience.

There was a moment of silence as James processed what just happened. He looked the figure over. It had the outline of a human's body but little else. There were no facial features either, just a tall, black silhouette.

It waved a hand in James's face. "Hello, anyone home?"

After staring back in silence for a moment longer, James replied with an awkward, "What?"

"Oh, so you *can* hear me," the figure quipped. "That's good, cause for a moment I was worried I accidentally turned you into a vegetable."

James' voice cracked with fear. "Uh, who are you?"

The figure chuckled. "Don't worry about that. I'm no one of consequence." The being sat down on the bed next to him and pointed at his face. "What's more important is who *you* are."

Eyes widening, James asked, "What do you mean?"

"I know what you were thinking of doing, James. I'm here to keep you from making the worst mistake of your life."

"Mistake?" James mumbled under his breath. Speaking louder, he asked, "What are you talking about?"

"Oh, do you need me to refresh your memory? Did you or did you not consider hurling yourself off a cliff not twelve hours ago?" Making a hand gesture, it imitated a person jumping from a ledge.

"What?" James barked. "How did you even know that? What are you?"

The figure started prancing around the room; it clearly had a flair for the dramatic. "Think of me as a friend, a friend who can help you get the thing you want most in the world." Now looking over his collection of manga, the figure remarked, "You read a lot of comics for a man your age. Did you know that?"

James let out a snicker. He was still not convinced this was happening. "No, no, no, you're just some weird figment of my imagination. This is just an odd dream, and I'm going to wake up any moment and laugh about how absurd it all was."

The figure danced over, imitating a new move that had taken the internet by storm, and pinched James on the shoulder.

"Ow!"

"Sorry, friend, but this isn't a dream. I have been watching you for a while. I wasn't going to reveal myself to you just yet, but after what happened yesterday, I figured I needed to move quickly. I want to make a deal with you."

James sat there processing the surreal exchange. An odd, otherworldly figure had appeared in his room stating it wanted to make a deal? "Are you some kind of devil?" he asked bluntly.

The figure laughed uproariously. "No, no, I'm no devil. I'm just a friend who sees what you're going through and wants to offer a helping hand."

"A friend who sees what I'm going through. You have no idea what my life is like!"

Turning its head to the side, the figure began to list off a number of uncanny details. "Let's see,

James Jeffords was born in the year 3449 to Alfred and Malinda Jeffords. You got subpar grades as you went through school and ended up dropping out of college, working several factory jobs until you finally settled at your current mode of employment. You have had 3 girlfriends in your life, 4 if you include the time you kissed Stacy Albright in the second grade, which, by the way, I wouldn't count. Moving on to the present you are hopelessly depressed with no purpose whatsoever. Did I miss anything?"

Mouth agape, James replied, "No...I think you summed it up rather well."

"At least you're not that ugly," The being reassured.

"Right, cause you're clearly an authority on appearance," James jeered. "No offense, but you look like every child's worst nightmare."

The figure looked itself up and down. "Are you trying to body-shame me?"

It sauntered back over and sat down on the bed. "Look, kid, I don't have a physical form. This is all just being projected into your brain for your own sake. Have you ever tried speaking to someone who can't see you? They think they're going nuts."

"Hold on, if you don't have a body, then how did you pinch me?"

It slid a finger across James' forehead. "I know how your tiny little meat sack of a mind works, and I can make you feel just about anything I want. For example, is it getting warmer in here?"

Suddenly, James felt like he was burning up. Once he started to cry out in pain, the figure snapped its fingers, and the burning sensation vanished.

"So, what do you want with me?" James wondered.

The being let out a long sigh. "It's complicated, but I can try to summarize. You and I want the same thing: to change this world for the better. The thing is, neither of us can do that without each other's help."

James thought about what it was saying. He still was not convinced that all this was really happening, but he decided to play along. "Why choose me? Isn't there someone much more powerful like a superhero you could team up with?"

"Actually, no," the figure replied despondently. "I can only bind myself to a person that has the same kind of – how do I say this – life force as mine. Every person has a signature and ours must be compatible for the bond to take hold."

James could sense the desperation in its tone. It was a desperation he could relate with. "So, there is no one else you can be bothering for this?"

The figure shook its head.

"So, what do I get if I do bind with you? You said that we can give each other what we want. How would that work?"

It placed a hand on James' chest and sent a wave of empowering sensations through his body. "I can give you the ability to do incredible things. In time, you will have powers no hero on this planet could ever dream of obtaining."

It removed its hand from him and let James catch his breath. "But why do you want to help me save this world? What investment do you have in it?"

"Honestly, my people forbid engaging with other species. The thing is, I always enjoyed being around creatures like you much more than I do my own kind. I have seen firsthand the pain that greed and power run amuck can cause. All I want is to help save your planet from that kind of fate."

"And what's the catch?" James asked cautiously. He knew deals like this always had fine print. Panels from his comic books popped into his head, specifically the one where Captain Charisma makes a deal with Doctor Delinquent thinking he had pure intentions when in reality he was using him for evil ends.

"No catch. I get what I want, you get what you want. Nothing I said is a lie, on this I swear." The figure moved in closer and put out his hand for a shake. "Sound good to you?"

James hesitated. None of this seemed real, and even if it was, it all sounded crazy. At the same time, it was the answer to his dreams. "I'm not sure about this."

Nodding as though it understood, the being patted him on the leg and said, "I don't blame you for being cautious. You just haven't been able to open your heart ever since your dog, cat, and hamster ran away, have you?"

"It's just that it happened all in the same day, that's what made it so difficult!" James bemoaned while holding back a tear. All things considered, he decided to give it a shot. After all, what did he have left to lose? *Certainly not my dog,* he mused. However, before he could agree, there was one more thing he needed to know: "What's your name?" he asked the odd being.

It chuckled, humored by how much stock humans put in a person's designation. "Kazav," it replied as disarmingly as possible.

"Nice to meet you," James remarked. "And you swear that nothing bad will happen if we do this?"

"I swear," the figure promised as it held its hand to its chest.

James' movement was restored, and he sat up in his bed, looking out at the dark hand being held in front of him. After considering things once more, he extended his own hand and clasped it firmly.

"Excellent!" Kazav exclaimed. He then began to glow, getting brighter as he cast beams of blinding light across the room.

James' arm burned and tingled like a million needles were passing through it and racing into his heart. Kazav faded as he transferred himself into James through the handshake they shared. Reality bent and distorted. James' vision blurred, and an immense ringing pierced into his skull.

The intensity of the moment overwhelmed him. One last flash of light burst out as Kazav completed the transfer. James fell back onto his bed, his consciousness fading until he passed into a deep, dark sleep.

The room was silent, with no other sounds other than the ticking of the clock and James' intermittent snoring. All, it seemed, was back to normal.

2/AWAKENING

The next thing James saw was the ceiling as he opened his eyes and groaned. He sat up in his bed and fought to keep himself from falling back asleep.

Just as his head hit the pillow, he sprung up in a panic as the events of the night came rushing back. He looked all around the room for signs someone might have been in it, but nothing looked out of the ordinary. Not that anything could stand out amid the piles of clothes and drawer tops full of useless junk.

"Hello?" he called out into the room. "Kazav?"

There was no answer. After a few minutes of waiting, he decided that the entire thing must have been a bad dream brought about by all the stress and anxiety he had been feeling. *Maybe I'm finally going insane,* he joked to himself, though it wouldn't surprise him.

In any case, he had to get going for work. There was no time to eat or shower. He had to go now, or he would be late again. He threw on some clothes he picked up from the floor and headed out the door. Work was a five-minute walk from his place, and he had to make sure he didn't get stopped by all the crosswalks. Sometimes he felt like they were scheduled in a way to purposefully make him tardy.

As he was walking down the street, a man walking his dog was approaching James from the opposite direction. Animals usually loved James, perhaps picking up on his sadness, but this time the dog started growling the closer he got. As they passed by, the man had to pick the dog up in his arms to keep it from lunging out at James.

"I'm so sorry!" the man shouted. "He never acts like this. Bad Mr. Woofers!"

Great. Now dogs don't like me either.

It wasn't just dogs. While walking by one of his neighbor's homes, all the stray cats that sat on the porch hissed at him. He timidly hurried past them before they got any ideas.

Eventually, he got to the final intersection he always crossed when heading to work. He had held this job for over a year, which was longer than he stayed at most. It was a factory that made kitchen appliances and hardware. He hated it, to say the least.

Normally, his job wore him out, and by the end of the day, he usually couldn't feel his legs from all the standing, crouching, and lifting he had to do. Oddly enough, today was different. When his shift ended, he still felt like he had the energy to keep working. He almost, dare he say it, enjoyed himself.

The clock struck 4 p.m. and like every day, he rushed out of the factory along with all the other clinically depressed people who called that place their job.

Not only did he make the most units he had ever done in one day, breaking the factory record, but he didn't even break a sweat. Where normally a frown adorned his face, a smile popped up instead.

Outside the factory, toward the main doors, something caught his attention. There was a crowd of people standing in a circle and shouting over one another while trying to get to the center. James stepped up on his tippy toes to try and find the cause of the commotion.

A superhero had defeated a small monster that had been lurking around the neighborhood. People were trying to get autographs and pictures with the man before he left.

James looked on for a moment, staring at the sad, tiny monster lying under the hero's boot. It was a scrawny little thing with big ugly black eyes and a mangled-looking body. Its arms were like hooves, and it was pale and bloated. The hero, on the other hand, was the figure of perfection. Handsome, tall, ripped body – they even had a smile that gleamed white as pearls.

He was small-time, though. The small-time heroes trying to earn a place in the world still had to do something before they could be accepted in the big leagues. But besides petty crimes or defeating tiny runts, most heroes didn't do anything worthwhile. They put on a show, to be sure, but that's about it. A loud crack and boom echoed through the streets as the hero blasted off into the sky and disappeared.

"I suppose he was done getting everyone's admiration," James mumbled sullenly.

After arriving home, he dropped his keys and phone on the counter and started microwaving his dinner. Tonight, it was frozen mashed potatoes and meatloaf. He flipped on the TV and watched the news for a bit. More of the same old stories. Crime this and death that, someone was missing, or someone was on the run.

James finished eating and tried to throw the container away, but the trash was full, and he couldn't step it down any further than he already had. With no choice left, he bagged it up and headed outside to toss it.

He went to the dumpster and was about to throw out the bag when he noticed something out of the corner of his eye. It scurried behind him and dove into the bushes before he could get a good look. He figured it was a cat or maybe the raccoons that sometimes get into the trash, but this thing was grunting and panting like nothing he had ever heard before.

Slowly, he moved toward the bushes, anxious to see what was hiding within. "Don't worry," James said as calmly as he could. "I'm not going to hurt you. You can come on out."

He peeled back the leaves and let out a scream when out jumped the ugliest thing he had ever seen.

It was a monster. Not a big one, but a monster all the same.

"Woah, woah!" he shouted as his heart pounded in his chest.

He tried moving back in a slow, steady manner to keep from spooking it. The monster wasn't big, but it still had fangs, claws, and one nasty attitude. Once James hit the back wall where the door to the building was, he tried feeling for the handle without taking his eyes off the creature. It started walking forwards, growling, and getting nastier by the second.

"Easy, easy, little fellow."

His attempts to calm it failed, and the beast lunged, throwing its entire body against James. He struggled to pull it off as the monster grabbed hold and bared its wretched teeth. He punched it in the face and eyes, trying to get it to back away, but it dug its claws into his side and latched on. James screamed in pain as the sharp talons pierced his ribs.

They spun around in the alley as James tried flinging it off him. After giving it a few hard punches in the back of the head, it jumped off, hissing at him all the while. James winced and gripped his side with one hand. Blood turned his shirt crimson.

The creature jolted toward him again, only this time James was prepared. Just as it got close enough, he drew his leg back and kicked the creature with everything he had.

A loud crack rang out into the alley as the force of the kick caused the creature to go flying out into the sky. It fell before long and disappeared behind another building as it landed.

James took a moment to catch his breath and then ran inside to call for help. He clambered up the stairs until he got to his apartment door and immediately called the authorities.

They asked him all the standard questions. *What happened? Where are you? Are you injured?*

He answered everything, but just as he was going to inform them that he had been stabbed, he paused.

"Sir," the operator repeated. "Are you injured?"

He wasn't sure what to say – his wound no longer existed. "Um, um, I suppose. I mean, I guess." Unable to find his wound, he stopped rambling and just said, "No, I'm not injured."

"Excellent, we will inform the local police as well as the local Heroes Guild, and they will take care of things from here. Stay safe, citizen. Goodbye, and thank you for your call."

The line clicked as the call ended. James sat there confused. There was still blood on him, but no open wound.

That's when a mischievous voice teased, *Impressive, isn't it?*

James jerked from the surprise and looked around but couldn't see anyone else here with him.

The voice let out a little chuckle before saying, *I think you and I need to have a little chat, kid.*

3/SMALL BEGINNINGS

James looked around the room, trying to pinpoint where the voice was coming from.

Don't bother looking for me, Kazav mocked. *I'm in your head, and it's ugly in here.*

James shook his head. "I finally lost it, didn't I? The stress of that attack was the cherry on the cake that is my insanity, wasn't it?"

I can't speak for your mental health, kid, but I assure you you're not hearing things. Nope, I'm as real as rain.

"So last night wasn't just some crazy stress dream? You really are all up in my brain?"

Bingo!

James looked down at where his wound was. "So, this was all because of you? How did you do that?"

You and I are now bound – mind, body, heart, and soul. What happens to you happens to me and vice versa. But unlike you, I have the power to regenerate your primitive body at a rate much quicker than you could on your own.

"So, you healed me?"

Yup, and that's not all! Did you even see how far you kicked that little freak? I'd like to see you get that kind of air without my help.

"What exactly does this all mean? Am I invincible?"

Ha! Not even close! Here is how this is going to work. The more you use my abilities, the stronger our bond will grow, and the more of my power will be at your disposal. But I'm not limitless. If you take too much damage all at once, I might not be able to save you. So, start small and hone your abilities. Then, after you have built up some more power, we can start tackling bigger issues.

"What issues did you have in mind?"

Don't worry about it. There will be time to talk about all that when we can actually do something about it. For now, I recommend you break in your new abilities.

James looked down at his hands. "How do I do that?"

Just start running around, jump off a building, punch some stuff, I don't know, just do what you always wished you could do.

James ran down to the stairwell and decided his first test would be jumping off the top. Being ten feet, it could easily cause injury should he land wrong.

He leaped and landed on the ground below. He braced for pain, but once his feet touched the ground, he didn't feel a thing.

C'mon, is that the best you can do? Kazav goaded.

Go jump off the roof of the apartment. I promise you can handle it.

James froze at the thought. "Seriously?"

Seriously.

He ran up to the roof, ten flights of stairs, without even needing to catch his breath. Once he got up there and leaned over the ledge, he started having doubts.

Well, I'm waiting.

James gulped as his throat tightened with fear. "It's just that it looks a lot higher than I was expecting."

Well, then it looks like I'm going to have to give you some encouragement.

James' legs jerked forward, and he flung off the roof headfirst. He let out a bloodcurdling scream as he fell, which came to a stop once he hit the ground. He lay their motionless, his eyes unblinking, mouth agape.

But after a few moments, he realized he was fine. There wasn't a scratch on him and not a single broken bone. He looked over his body in awe and let out a relieved laugh.

Kazav snickered. *Pretty sweet, huh? Sorry, I had to give your legs a spasm.*

"That was amazing!" James exclaimed. "But don't ever, and I mean *ever*, do that again. Do you understand?"

Fine, fine. I won't push you anymore, I promise.

James jumped up and looked for something else to do. "Can I punch that rock?"

Sure, I mean, it's not exactly thinking big, but go nuts. Punch a million rocks, for all I care.

He ran over and hit the rock with all his might. He took a tiny chunk out of it without harming his fist.

Wow, you showed that inanimate object whose boss, didn't you? Kazav jeered.

"This is amazing! I can't believe this is happening!"

Kazav laughed at James for being so excited. This wasn't even a fraction of what he would be able to do, and yet he was so elated.

Humans are funny, Kazav mused.

James looked out into the street.

"I'm gonna go for a run!" he announced as he took off into a sprint. He had tried running in the past when he was trying to get in shape but could never make it past a few blocks before getting winded and giving up.

James cleared 5 blocks until he circled the main road and headed back to the apartments. "That was amazing! I feel like I could run for hours!"

That's small potatoes compared to what we'll be able to do in the near future, kid.

He stayed out the rest of the day as he broke in his new abilities. Elation and excitement ran high.

While he sprinted around, feeling boundless, James took in a breath of air and could swear it had never smelled so sweet.

————

The next morning, Kazav woke James with a shrill screech that echoed through his skull, forcing him to sit up in bed and hold his hands up to his ears.

"Gaaah!" he cried out as he shook his head.

Rise and shine! Kazav shouted as loud as it could.

Agitated, James sat up and looked at the clock. "It's midnight. Didn't you ask me to get some sleep after all that running?"

Kazav chuckled. *You think monsters and villains wait until daylight? No! It's when the sun goes down that the real fun begins.*

James stood up and walked over to his closet. As he looked for something to wear, a thought sprang to mind. "Don't I need a costume or something? To protect my identity?"

Exactly who do you have to protect, James? You have no friends or family. Besides, don't you want people to know who you are?

Looking down at the floor, James let out a long, sad groan. "That's just the thing. Heroes used to have dignity and discretion. They didn't care about fame and recognition. They protected the world and asked for nothing in return. That's the way it should be."

James pulled out a playing card with an old superhero's image on the cover. The card read, *Quasar, the scourge of the underworld.* It was one in a series of collectibles.

Who's the dork? Kazav mocked.

"He's not a dork," James shot back. "This is Quasar. He was a famous superhero from before I was even born."

And this guy is your role model?

James nodded as he looked at the card with pride. "This guy was the real deal. He saved the city more times than you could count, and, in the end, he gave his life to protect it. That's what being a hero is all about."

Kazav huffed. It was unconvinced. *Sounds like a lot of sentimental drivel if you ask me.*

James' face scrunched up. Kazav's snide remarks were starting to bug him. "Are you telling me you hate goodness? Isn't the reason you're helping me because you want to make the world a better place?"

I do want to make this world better. But that doesn't mean I'm not a realist. There are many roads to the same goal, and many different definitions of what goodness is. Try not to forget that.

James snorted in disagreement. "Sounds pretty pessimistic if you ask me."

Kazav gave no reply. James tucked the photo back into the drawer and rummaged through his closet.

We should get going, kid, crime won't fight itself.

He threw on a hoodie and jeans; it was the closest thing to a hero outfit he was going to get. "Where are we going anyway?"

The park. Trust me, after-dark parks become cesspools of crime and monster activity.

"That's a sad statement."

Sad but true. Now get going! Also, put on a darker hoodie so you blend in with the night!

James zipped up the only black hoodie he had and darted out the window. He landed on his feet from five stories up.

Still so cool, he thought to himself while looking up at his third-story window. He made his way through the city until he reached the entrance to the park. It was dimly lit by two streetlamps that barely illuminated the welcome sign.

"Now what?" James asked Kazav, who had barely spoken a word the entire journey.

Go inside and run around until you find something heroic to do. Trust me, it won't take long.

James entered and kept along the cobblestone path that ran on the perimeter of the park. It amazed him how different everything was now that his senses were heightened. Every sight, sound, and smell, no matter how insignificant, was clear as day!

He roamed for an hour or so before a shrill scream rang out from across the park.

"Monster! Help! Monster!" a woman screeched into the night.

With that, James ran off at full speed. He moved

like a cheetah, darting over benches and zigzagging in between trees with a fluid grace he had never known. In no time, he found the cause of all the screaming.

A scaly, ugly, lizard-like creature was chasing a woman in a tattered dress. It was snapping at the air and reaching its claws out to try and grab her.

It's go time! Kazav shouted. *Bring that beast to its knees!*

James launched from behind the trees and slammed his body into the creature. The woman looked back at them and then kept on running until she disappeared into the darkness. The force of the impact caused both James and the creature to roll across the ground and come to a stop against a massive tree trunk.

The beast jumped up from the ground lightning-quick and lashed out with massive, clawed arms. James kicked the tree and slid across the ground away from it just in time to dodge its claws. With his hands, James flipped off the ground and onto his feet. He looked to where the monster was but didn't see it anymore. It had already moved in from behind and was closing its massive jaws around him.

His eyes went wide as he saw the rows of razor-sharp teeth about to snap shut and end it all. Just as its teeth pierced his skin, James let off a reflexive punch that connected with the creature's stomach and forced it down the path.

The monster dug its claws into the ground to slow its speed, ripping up the pavement as it was pushed back from the force of the blow. James went on the offensive and launched a barrage of kicks and punches at the beast in hopes of putting a quick end to the battle. Each hit collided with the lizard's rock-hard scales, forcing out pained grunts and hisses with every strike.

The park grounds became a battlefield as fists and claws, flesh and scales went toe to toe in life-or-death combat. For every hit that James landed on the creature, it was able to land one back.

James was hurt, but so was the creature. His powerful blows were starting to have a serious effect. It looked like the monster was almost done for as it kneeled in pain. James used the moment to launch another series of blows against it but was taken by surprise as it let out a glob of steaming venom from its festering maw and hurled it at James' face. He managed to dodge the toxic goo, but it left him wide open. The lizard whipped him with its tail, sending him headfirst into a stone fountain. He lay there in a daze, his vision splitting.

C'mon, kid, you gotta get up! Kazav shouted to try and rouse him.

"My head," James grumbled through clenched teeth.

It's heading back over! You don't have time to lay on the ground!

His vision was blurred. He could only vaguely

see the outline of the monster hulking toward him.

If you don't move, it could be all over! Kazav screamed in a panic.

James was barely conscious as he stumbled back and forth. The monster had now made its way over to him and wrapped its tail around his body in a vice-like grip. James cried out in pain as the tail constricted like a boa around its prey.

The monster brought a hand up and was ready to strike the killing blow.

Just before the lizard claws reached his neck, a rock came flying out of the darkness and hit it square in the eye. It recoiled and let out a hiss, dropping James as it rubbed a swollen eye.

The silhouette of a woman could be seen chucking rocks and sticks at the creature, helping to draw its attention away from James.

Now's your chance! Kazav urged. *Take him down*!

With an ear-rending cry and a surge of adrenaline, James gave it everything he had. Taking hold of the lizard's tail, he ripped it clean off the creature's body and threw it on the ground. It slithered around like a snake, twitching despite being separated from its master.

The creature was now in a daze and had lost all sense of balance. Still in a rage-fueled stupor, James launched off the ground and whipped his foot out at the monster, sending it flying until it collided with a metal gate that made up the park's outer wall.

Great job, kid!

Kazav's applause turned into a muffled blur of jumbled words, and James teetered as he stood, dizziness now overwhelming him. The only thing he could hear was Kazav's garbled voice as he fell over and sank into darkness.

4/NEW FRIENDS

James awoke to the rhythmic beeping of an electrocardiogram machine. The smells and sounds gave no room for uncertainty – he was in the hospital. An IV line dangled from his wrist up to the bag of saline hanging by a hook above him. Nurses and doctors shouted to one another as patients were rushed up and down the halls. The pale white walls and decorations gave the deceiving impression of hope and light in a place that rarely contained either.

James tried sitting up in his bed but didn't have the strength to move.

"What happened?" he groaned.

We overdid it, kid. Kazav replied, a worried tone in his voice.

James winced as he tried to move his arms. "What do you mean?"

You took more damage than I thought. That lizard thing did a number on you.

"But I thought you could heal me from stuff like that."

I did what I could, but our bond is still new. I don't have the best reading on your limits yet.

James looked under his gown and saw the bruises and claw marks peppering his body. It looked worse than it felt thanks to Kazav blocking the pain.

Look on the bright side: you survived your first fight! From here on out, you can only grow stronger.

James started poking at a bump on his head. "Really?"

It's like I said, kid, the more you use your new abilities, the stronger our bond becomes, and the stronger you become.

The door to the room swung open and in walked a doctor. He placed a chart down on the table next to the bed and introduced himself. "Hello James, my name is Doctor Ankari. You are in the hospital after what looks to be a monster attack." The doctor sat down and pulled the glasses hanging from his neck over his eyes. As he looked over a clipboard, he asked, "Can you tell me what happened?"

Kazav chimed in before James could say anything: *Don't tell him everything. Just tell him enough.*

James gathered his thoughts and then offered an explanation. "I was walking through the park last night and I-" He paused for a moment, trying to flesh out the details. "I must have been attacked or something. It all happened so fast. I'm not sure I remember anything else."

The doctor nodded and gave him an empathetic look. "That's very common in cases like this." He looked over the chart again and asked, "There was an eyewitness who says you managed to fight off the attacker. Do you remember anything regarding that?"

James shook his head. "Sorry, it's all just a blur."

The doctor nodded again, then sat up. "Well, we would typically keep a patient with your injuries for at least a few days; however, your recovery is moving incredibly fast." Looking on the other side of the chart, he asked, "You're not a hero, are you?"

James' eyes narrowed. "No, why do you ask?"

"It's just that your last name sounds so familiar." The doctor snapped his fingers and asked, "You're not related to the hero Dauntless, are you?"

James' face scrunched up anytime he heard that name. "He is my –" A lump formed in his throat. He swallowed it and mumbled, "Brother."

"Amazing!" the doctor exclaimed. "You don't think I could get his autograph, do you?"

James sneered at the doctor with a look that could kill. "That would require I talk to him. So no, you can't have his autograph."

There was an awkward pause as they both stared in silence.

"Anyway, you seem to be on the mend, but we still want to keep you here until you make a full recovery. A nurse will be in soon to check on you." The doctor hung the clipboard on the door and left the room, giving James the freedom to let out an exacerbated sigh.

Kazav was curious as to why James had such

a negative reaction when the doctor brought up his brother. *What's wrong, sport?*

"I don't like when people ask me about Jeremy."

Why? Are you jealous?

James snorted. "Of course! But you know, it's so much more than that. I grew up with him and knew him as my brother before he became the Amazing Dauntless and I know for a fact that he's nothing like the kind and charming hero he pretends to be."

Kazav's interest was piqued. *What's he really like?*

As James thought about his childhood, memories came flooding back. All the good, all the bad, mostly the bad. "He was just...different, that's all."

Don't want to talk about it, huh? I know how you feel. Back where I'm from, all I ever did was let people down. I failed in some big ways, and I'm still learning to live it down.

James took a small bit of comfort in the fact that even a being like Kazav had things it regretted. Maybe he wasn't such a failure after all.

The next twelve hours went by slow. James took the time to absorb everything that had happened the past few days. He realized he hadn't really thought about just how bizarre his new situation was. He also chatted with Kazav and tried to pry it for information, but it was stingy on the details. James was hoping to learn more about where Kazav came from but was getting the cold shoulder. They watched cartoons for the next few hours and ate a disgusting hospital meal that made his reheated dinners seem fit for a king.

At the end of the day, the doctor came back to examine James' wounds. "Huh, you must have some of your brother's blood because you heal unusually quick! With progress like this, I don't see a reason to keep you overnight. I'll have the nurse begin the discharge papers."

In no time, James was out of the hospital and on his way back home for some peace and quiet. However, once he rounded the corner to the street his apartment was on, he noticed he was being followed. Every time he turned around to try and get a look at who it was, they vanished.

James couldn't tell what was after him, but he wasn't in the mood for another fight. He shot into a sprint, bolting down the street as fast as he could. The entire time he was running, it felt like something was closing in, ready to reach out and grab him.

He made it to the apartment and burst through the doors. Panic coursed through his veins as he ran up the stairs and into the hallway his unit was on. He dashed to the door, opened it, and slammed it shut, bolting all three of the locks he had installed.

Then, turning around, he let out a startled and somewhat embarrassing screech as he saw a group of shadowy figures emerge from the darkness of his living room.

"Hello," a mysterious voice called through the darkness. "We have been waiting for you."

James reached for the light beside him and flipped the switch. With the room fully illuminated, the strangers came into clear view. A woman – a hero – sat on his sofa next to two others. James knew from appearance alone who they were.

"Are you Shadow Sparrow?" he asked, pointing to the woman in the middle.

She sat up and walked towards him. "Indeed, although I go by Sparrow for short," she cooed, tossing her jet-black hair behind her head with a flick of her wrist

James took a moment to analyze her costume. It was a purple fabric that hugged her body. Black and blue lines followed down her arms and legs and ended at her hands. She had an insignia of an eagle on her chest. A piece of armored black leather shielded her torso and matched her gloves. She was, by all accounts, intimidating.

"More to the point is who *you* are," she remarked as she poked him in the chest with her finger. If there was one thing Sparrow loved, it was getting down the fine print. Finding out what made a person tick be they hero or villain.

James was bewildered by her presence and stuttered. "W-what do you mean?"

"Please," she scoffed. "Nothing goes down in this neighborhood without us knowing about it. We know what you did to King Lizard, the monster that's been haunting the park." She pointed to the guy sitting on the left seat of the couch. "Falcon over there saw everything. He was the one who took you to the hospital after you passed out."

He gave James a finger gun and a wink.

Finger gunning back, James asked, "Thanks, I guess, but what are you doing in my apartment?"

"Our sector has been hunting for recruits for some time. We saw how you handled that scaled abomination and wanted to offer you a chance to join our squad."

He raised an eyebrow. The offer was intriguing. "Why the house call? Don't you have hundreds of recruits to choose from?"

A frown grew on her face, slowly morphing into a pout. James could see charm was one of the weapons in her arsenal. That, and rifling through his belongings apparently. All his cabinets, drawers and desks had been emptied, their contents strewn about.

Kicking a path clear, she replied, "Not anymore. Most novice heroes flock to the inner city where the rankings and fame are more lucrative. None of them care about protecting their community." An outcome that aggravated her to no end.

Falcon chimed in by saying, "That's why we do this low-key. We only want to recruit people who care about the city and the people who call it home."

James nodded along as they spoke. What they were saying certainly lined up with his values. Still, they were a part of the Guild, and that made them hard to trust. "You claim you care about the people of the city, but most of the heroes I know are attention-seeking phonies. How do you know I'm worth your time?

Falcon and Sparrow smirked at one another – they liked the question. "We don't. That's why you're going to prove it to us. Pass our test, and you can join the Guild. Decline, and we won't bother you anymore."

James stroked his chin as he considered the offer. He hadn't thought about joining the local Guild as he still considered heroes to be part of the problem. That being said, they seemed like the real deal, Sparrow in particular. James watched her as she sauntered about, examining every detail of his apartment. Her eyes cast a focused, mysterious gaze upon all they observed, a quality that made James feel more than a little self-conscious.

"Do I have to answer right now?" James asked Sparrow as she rifled through a magazine that he had left out on the coffee table.

"How about this: if you take down the monster called Black Octopus, we will consider that an acceptance of our offer."

James chuckled when he heard the name. "Who, or what, is Black Octopus?"

Falcon stood up and gave James a rundown. "It's a local monster that has been living in the sewers beneath the streets. He comes out at night and drags anything down into the sewer he can get his tentacles on. Deer, pets, bikes, and recently, people."

"You take him down," Sparrow purred, "and you can join us."

She pointed to the window and ordered her teammates to leave. Now outside on the sidewalk, Sparrow looked up at James and said, "By the way, I'm not sure why you chose to keep your power a secret for so long, but don't worry, I won't tell your brother." And just like that, she disappeared into the night.

Now that they were alone, Kazav offered his thoughts. *I'm not sure about this. Didn't you want to change the entire way the Guild operates? Joining them might shift your goals.*

"You're right. On the other hand, they do seem different than what I was expecting."

Maybe so, but here is something to consider. They may be your allies now, but the second your goals change, or you have to do something that puts you outside their definition of morals, you're going to have to pick a side.

James' concern grew the more Kazav spoke. "What do you mean by that?"

Just be careful who you align yourself with. I'll support whatever choice you make, kid, but make it with a view to the long-term. Do you understand?

"Um, I think so."

Silence fell again until it was interrupted by James' howling stomach.

"Man, I'm starving!" James made the biggest sandwich he could.

Kazav tried to hold back a laugh as he watched

James practically inhale his food.

"What's so funny?"

It just amuses me how much humans love food. I mean, you work for it, you pay for it, you assemble it, and then you rip it apart with your tiny little teeth. It's funny, is all.

"Well, what exactly do you eat?"

I don't eat in the same sense that you do, kid. I don't have a body, but I still need one to exist. Once the person I'm paired with dies, then I begin to weaken. Eventually, I am forced back to my home planet. That's why I had to bond with you in the first place. It's not just out of the goodness of my heart, but rather out of survival.

"How were you born, then? Do you have a mother or father?"

Kazav let out an agitated grumble. *I'd rather not get off-topic. Let's just focus on what our next move is. You need to gain strength and to do that, you need to challenge yourself. So, whether you decide to join that little kiddy club or not, we have a good lead on your next target. We need to find that Black Octopus thing in the sewers and take it out.*

James' face soured as he imagined walking around in the dirty, murky waters. "You want me to go trudging around in the sewers? What if I get an infection?"

You can't get infections anymore, you dunce. Now get some rest. You have a big day ahead of you.

5/BLACK OCTOPUS

Thick globs of muck and waste stuck to the walls of the sewer drain that James was venturing through. Rats scurried across the floor, and cockroaches carpeted the ceiling.

"This is disgusting." James gagged.

It's even worse now that your senses are heightened, Kazav gleefully informed him.

Every step James took sounded like someone trudging through watery mud and every breath he took was foul enough to knock out an elephant.

"Are you sure we should even be down here? Can't we find a more scent-friendly target?"

Not if you want to join that band of merry men who showed up last night, we can't. Now stop whining and focus up. I think I see some tracks.

"By the way, Kazav, I have been meaning to ask more about how our powers work."

Ask away.

"Do you see through my eyes? Can you smell what I smell? Hear what I hear? And so on?"

I can choose to use your senses if I want, but I'm not limited to your body's perceptions. I can sense things that you simply never could and send that information to your brain. That's why you can smell, hear, see, and feel in a way you never could before.

"If that's how it works, could you turn my ability to smell off? At least until we leave the sewers?"

Kazav chuckled. *I could, but I* won't.

James was about to object to Kazav's somewhat sadistic sense of humor when something caught his eye. There were tracks in the tunnel that branched off from the one they were currently exploring. Strange footprints, as well as slide marks, as though something were being dragged behind.

Bingo! Kazav exclaimed.

James entered the new tunnel and followed the footprints as the paths forked and split. Bones, muck, and random trinkets littered the floor along with torn clothes and a small pile of wallets and purses.

I think we found all those missing people, Kazav remarked cautiously. *Keep going, kid, but be careful.*

James went even deeper into the sewer until he entered a large room with tunnels leading off in every direction.

"Now what?" James whispered. The sound of his voice echoed off the dank sewer walls and branched out into each passage.

Before Kazav could reply, a low rumble reverberated around the chamber. It was like the base of a speaker blasting out through a subway tunnel.

The hair on James' neck stood on end as the grumbling grew closer and the sound of bones crunching under footsteps grew louder and louder. He took a battle stance and steeled his nerves for whatever might come be coming to meet them. The grumbling increased, and as the noise resonated across the room, it became impossible to tell which way it was coming from. Just as the sound grew loudest, it stopped as if whatever was making it just disappeared.

Tension grew the longer the silence went on, and James began to shake with a mix of anxiety and anticipation. Not a second later, an overwhelming urge to duck took hold of him. He obeyed and narrowly avoided a massive black tentacle that came swinging out from behind. He turned to face his attacker and almost dry-heaved at its appearance.

Crawling from the ceiling, dripping with slime and sewage, was a half-man, half octopus-like being. It let out a deafening screech and extended every one of its foul tentacles out into the air.

James was planning to strike, but the monster beat him to it and sent out its slimy tentacles with deadly speed. The air whizzed as they passed by James' head. Shot after shot, stretch after stretch, the creature kept hurling its limbs, seeking to grab James and devour him with its festering jaws.

James could dodge them well enough but couldn't get close enough to get in a strike. What good would his newfound strength be if he spent all his energy just trying to not get hit?

Kazav offered a timely suggestion: *Try getting behind it. It doesn't look like it has any kind of defense in the rear!*

James leaped over the creature and used the wall behind as a launching pad. With full force, he aimed for the beast's back, pulling his arm back to ready the strike.

Just as his fist was clenched and ready to go, the monster spun and countered with another tentacle slap. James grunted as his body slammed into the stone walls of the sewer, crashing through the ancient bricks and sending them to the ground below.

To his surprise, it didn't hurt as much as he was expecting. Kazav was keeping on top of things and made sure James' back quickly recovered from the force of the blow.

Picking up a stone from the floor, James hurled it at the monster's face. It acted as an effective distraction, allowing him to bolt and ready another strike. The beast blindly sent out a wave of its tentacles in hopes of stopping him, but they met empty air.

James was now directly in front of the beast and had already initiated a devastating blow. The monster had time to see, but not avoid, the fist closing in on its ugly face.

His hand connected with the monster's sticky skin and, with a loud *thwack*, sent it rocketing into the wall. It fell to the ground, covered in the rubble of the crumbling sewers. In imitation of James, it grabbed a stone in each tentacle, eight in total, and started throwing them like deadly missiles.

James dodged most of them but not all. A few stones struck his body, causing bruises to pepper his torso. "Not bad," James taunted. "But not good enough!"

He burst forward with every bit of speed he could muster. The monster sent out all of its wicked tentacles in an attempt to force him back, but James weaved and deflected whatever came near. The beast was shocked as every one of its attempts to strike him failed.

Like before, James was now too close for the monster to avoid yet another devastating hit. His clenched fist landed squarely against the monster's face and sent rippling shockwaves through its body. Digging its arms into the ground, it slowed its backslide and tried to get reoriented.

Whipping out a tentacle, it managed to land a hit, but James pushed through and sent out a machine-gun-like volley of blows. Fist after fist, smacking it further and further into the wall. The wall and ceiling started to give way, and sunlight peeked from the open sky above. With the light shining against the monster, James began to see just how hideous it truly was.

"Man, are you ugly!" he cried out as he lost focus.

That would prove to be a mistake, and the monster seized the lapse in action to grab James by the leg. It hung him upside down and brought him face to face. With a scowl, the beast roared at him, revealing rows of jagged yellow teeth. With a smooth flick of a tentacle, it sent him flying up and crashing through the street above.

People looked on in shock as the ground ripped apart in front of them and James shot through into the daylight, landing on the street. Cars fell in as the road sank and crashed into the hole that had been created. A woman was about to fall into the pit along with her car, but James rushed over and tore the door off her vehicle, pulling her to safety.

Oddly, the car started moving back up from the hole as if something was lifting it out. The car then shot forward, forcing James to throw the woman to safety. She was safe, but he had no time to avoid the collision and was sent flying back as the car struck and pinned him down.

James tried lifting the car off, but two tentacles grabbed his arms and forced him down onto the pavement. Then, using its other appendages, it lifted the car and smashed it against James repeatedly.

The monster didn't stop until there was nothing left to hit him with and then tossed the remaining chunks of the car off into the street. James struggled to get free as the monster wrapped more of its tentacles around him and started pulling in different directions. He could feel his bones clacking and expanding as the monster tried to rip him apart.

"Kazav! A little help would be nice!"

It's taking everything I have to keep your limbs from flying off, kid, you're gonna have to think of something on your own!

Hope seemed lost until a black square formed in midair behind the creature. A figure jumped out from within and kicked the monster in the back of the head, forcing it to drop James as it was sent forward.

Shadow Sparrow leaned over and offered him a hand, smirking as she asked, "Need some help?"

A wave of relief washed over him. "If you feel you have the time," he quipped.

Sparrow effortlessly avoided the tentacles like it was some chore she could do with a blindfold on. With a shadow blade forming in the air, she gripped it and sliced the monster's tentacles off one at a time, forcing the beast to cry out and scramble away. Forming yet another shadow object, she threw it at the beast and shackled it to the ground, denying it the option of escape. With a quick and merciless thrust, she dispatched the monster, bringing an end to its rampage of death and destruction.

James looked on in awe as she confidently strutted back to him and picked him up off the ground.

"Impressed?" she asked as she shut his gaping jaw.

"Uh, yeah, that was, wow!"

She gave him a wink. "Yeah, I know." Then, waving him over, she commanded, "Follow me."

Taking his hand, she led him through dark alleys and side streets on their way to her guild chapter. Piles of garbage and unknown substances coated the ground they walked on, causing their steps to make a sloshing noise.

James covered his nose as they passed by a dumpster. "This HQ of yours is further than I was hoping."

Sparrow looked back at him as they hurried along. "Well, normally we would have been there by now, but I don't think you could keep up with me if I moved any faster than this."

"What do you mean by that?" James asked playfully.

Sparrow made a face at him. It was one of disappointment. "Well, I was expecting you to do a little better against Black Octopus. It seems like your powers are not as refined as I was hoping. I doubt you would be able to match my speed if I just went off running."

James furrowed his eyebrows in protest. "Well, I guess there's only one way to find out."

She grinned at his challenge. "All right, but don't say I didn't warn you."

She took off in a blur and was down the street before James could even react.

"Well, get after her!" Kazav barked out.

"Right!" James shouted as he burst into a sprint.

He was keeping up with her, barely. She leaped

over cars, weaved between homes and buildings, and slid underneath trucks as they drove by in a display of obvious and confident ability. James didn't get fancy; he was just trying not to lose her. In his mad quest to prove himself, he ran into several trash cans, parked cars, and even a few pedestrians. He felt bad but was determined not to fall behind.

After a few minutes of high-speed navigation, Sparrow slowed down, and they reached the edge of the city. She came to a stop at a secluded, overgrown field that hardly had the makings of a superhero hide-out.

Sparrow looked back at James, who was covered in alley goo. "Not bad," she teased.

He huffed a bit as he caught up. "Thanks. I think the old lady I almost ran over would disagree." Looking around at the empty field, James asked, "Are you sure we're in the right place?"

Sparrow didn't answer. Instead, she walked out into the swaying grass, waving her hands as she stepped further away. A shadowy square appeared in the air above her and began spinning rapidly, causing gusts of wind to sweep across the vegetation.

Then, out of the shadow, a structure came into view. Like a mirage in the desert, it shimmered until it became clear as day. The winds died down, and Sparrow signaled for James to follow.

Slack jawed, he exclaimed, "Wow, that was incredible!"

She winked at him as they walked up the stone stairs, stopping once they approached the outer doors. The building looked old, sort of like an ancient temple. Stone and wood made up the beams that supported the entrance. Huge oak doors guarded the way in and opening them seemed like it would require immense strength.

Sparrow grabbed one of the doors in her hand and flung it open like it was made of cardboard. James grabbed the other door but could barely make it budge.

"My hands are slippery," he said defensively as he tried to save a shred of dignity. She let out a giggle and waved a finger for him to keep following.

The inside looked like a mix of modern and ancient decorating styles. Sconces lined the hallways, and the structure was made of old stone with etchings and murals along the surface. At the same time, modern tech and equipment were set up in all the rooms, with wires running the length of the ceiling.

His voice echoed off the walls as he spoke, lending the building an eerie aura. "Hey, Sparrow, why are you hidden away in a crypt? This seems like an odd place for a Heroes Guild. Aren't they usually high tech and fancy?"

Sparrow waited for it to die down and replied, "This was an ancient hero's guildhall. When we discovered the building, we didn't have the heart to remove the original design. We just do our best to work around it." She placed a hand against one of the old stone arches that made up a doorway. "It's got a charm that I would never dare change."

A simple charm, Kazav muttered sarcastically.

They passed a dining hall, an armory, and several bunk rooms until they got to a large metallic door. James could tell this was not a standard feature of the guildhall and had been installed much more recently.

"You're about to meet the rest of the team," Sparrow informed him as she typed in the password. "Let's just hope they like you."

The doors hissed and parted, revealing a modern-looking room full of high-tech equipment. Advanced computers and gadgets rested atop the smooth metal tables along with 3D holograms displaying all kinds of graphs and images. A long table sat in the center of the room with a handful of heroes watching on as he approached.

Sparrow walked him over and got everyone's attention. "Team, meet James, our newest potential recruit."

The heroes clapped after the introduction, making James blush. He never knew what to do when all eyes were on him.

"Now for the introductions. You already met Falcon and Hawk back at your apartment."

Falcon threw up a peace sign, and Hawk smacked him from behind.

"Hey, what's that for?" Falcon grumbled as he smacked him back.

"It's cheesy," Hawk replied as he gave James a welcoming nod.

Sparrow rolled her eyes and kept going. "Next to them is Owl."

"Greetings," Owl remarked without looking up as he flipped through a magazine titled *Bird Baths and Beyond.*

"And that little cutie is Super Static," Sparrow chirped as she pointed over to a young woman who had her feet up on the table.

James raised an eyebrow. "That's...an interesting name. It doesn't really follow the bird theme you have going on."

Super Static leaned up in her chair and teased, "The irony behind that is of all the people here, I'm the most likely to peck your eyes out if you bug me."

James let out a nervous chuckle. "Well then, I'll try not to get on your bad side."

"That's everyone," Sparrow inserted. Then, walking over to him, she asked, "What are you thinking, James? Are you ready to do something great with your life and join the Guild?"

He looked around the room and then back at Sparrow. "What does it mean if I do join you? What would I have to do?"

She walked over to the monitor and pointed to a map of the city. "It means devoting your life to defending this city. It means giving up the mundane, pointless life you lived until now and answering to a higher calling. It's about being part of a unit, a team, and a family. We look out for each other and take care of one another. That's what it's all about."

James was feeling a little torn. Everything Sparrow was saying spoke directly to him. Was this the best way forward, or should he blaze his own trail? He went back and forth with those questions until he realized he had another person's opinion to consider: Kazav's. It felt wrong for him to decide without getting its opinion first.

"Would it be okay if I went somewhere private to think things over?"

Sparrow snapped her finger and said, "Falcon, go ahead and take James to the empty room at the end of the hall."

As Falcon approached, the sound of countless knives jingled and rattled like he was one giant weapon. "Come with me," he instructed James, who followed pensively.

They both left, and the steel doors to the main hall hissed shut. After passing by several other rooms, they got to the end of the hall, and Falcon motioned for James to enter.

"Meet us back in the main hall when you're done thinking things over."

James nodded, and Falcon walked away only to circle back. "By the way, an opportunity like this doesn't come around every day. Sparrow thinks we can trust you, so do I, but don't join unless you really want this."

After shutting the door, James sat on the old, rickety bed in the corner of the room. It was dusty and uncomfortable, and the box spring creaked and squealed as he put his weight on it.

What are we thinking? Kazav asked, eager to hear his opinion.

James put his hands on his knees. "I was about to ask you the same question."

He started looking around at the room, and it became clear nobody had been in here for a long time. Old trophies and accolades littered the walls dated for over fifty years ago. He put a trophy he had picked up back on the dusty table it came from. "It looks like whoever had this room last never came back to clean it out."

Or, Kazav quipped, *he never made it back alive.*

James shuddered. Being a hero was dangerous, and the possibility of early death was all too real.

"What do you think I should do?" James asked, hoping Kazav could steer him in the right direction.

Honestly, kid, this is all up to you. I don't like organizations like this, but I will support whatever choice you make.

With that, he sat there in the silent, dusty room and weighed the options in his hands. Memories of his childhood flooded him, all the insecurities, all the pressures he faced. That's when James started thinking back to why he was who he was.

6/PAST AND PRESENT

James had the perfect home growing up. Green grass, white picket fence, a loving family, everything a young boy would need to feel happy. Inside the home, images flashed across a TV in the same room where a young boy, James, was playing. Blocks were scattered over the carpeted floor and coloring books lay sprawled out, ready to trip an unsuspecting passerby.

Mealtime was a pleasant experience. Mom, Dad, Jeremy, and James all sat at the table and talked about their day. Mom and Dad talked about their time at work and all the people that annoyed them, the tasks they had to do, normal stuff. Jeremy and James talked about school and all the bullies they avoided, homework they didn't do, normal stuff. This was just before life would become a nightmare for James.

Before Jeremy discovered his powers, he and James were very close. They stood up for each other and had each other's backs just like brothers should.

But that soon changed when one morning Jeremy was at the dining room table and was getting frustrated with his math homework. He kept trying to get the right answer to an equation on his homework, but math had never been his strong suit. Most things that required deep thinking were not his strong suit.

In anger, he smashed his fist into the table and splintered it in half.

After that, his parents took him to a local Heroes' Guild to be examined, and sure enough, they confirmed he had extraordinary abilities. They took James to get tested alongside his brother. He was ecstatic; the thought of him being a hero was all he could have ever wished for. He imagined him and his brother taking out monsters left and right, serving the public while wearing epic tights.

Unlike his brother, when James went to get tested, he failed. They stated he had no special resistance, no super strength, no hyper-intelligence. He was just a normal boy, with normal abilities.

Life got rough after that. His parents began to praise his brother constantly, and Jeremy became the child who could do no wrong, commit no sin, and make no mistake. His friends in school worshipped him, and he quickly rose to the position of most popular. Girls wanted to be with him, and guys wanted to be him.

Besides seeing each other briefly at home, they didn't speak. James often became the punchline for a joke as people talked about how unremarkable he was when compared to his brother. His parents never said the words, but James could tell he was second in their minds by their actions.

He started retreating inside himself and became depressed and resentful. He even hurt himself several times trying to prove that he too possessed superhuman power, but all he ever proved was how frail he was, how hurt he was, and how bitter he was becoming.

Friends, family, even romantic partners all saw James as lesser, a black sheep, and not worth the time. Meanwhile, his brother rocketed to the top of the superhero world. His abilities were legendary, his fame was worldwide, and he was among the most idolized and popular heroes to exist.

Eventually, James faded from everyone's memory. The result of all this was hatred and anger at the world and the way it worked. He dreamed of somehow, someday, being able to make a difference and prove them all wrong, to tear down the twisted thrones that society built for the heroes and the people that worshipped them.

That opportunity never felt like it would ever come. He never expected to meet a mysterious being like Kazav, to be offered the power he dreamed of his entire life. Now that he had it, he wasn't even sure of what to do with it.

Should he join the Heroes Guild and change it from the inside? Should he destroy it and teach the world a lesson? Or maybe he should become the very threat the world needed to face. These were all things racing through his mind while lying on that dusty bed in that stuffy room.

A long period of silence elapsed before James said anything. Amidst all these questions, one cropped up in his brain that threw all the rest on the back burner.

"Kazav," James called out into the silence of the cold, empty room. "Who are you?"

What do you mean? Kazav responded tentatively. The question made it bristle. It was many things but being openly vulnerable was not one of them.

"I mean, who are you?" James repeated. "What do you stand for? What do you believe in?"

It let out a long sigh. *That question isn't as simple as you think. If you humans find it hard to define yourselves, then it's thousands of times more complicated for a being like me to give you a satisfying answer.*

James squinted. He felt Kazav was trying to give him the runaround. "Just tell me more about you. What are your goals and ambitions? What is it that drives you forward?

Kazav groaned at the barrage of questions. It hated the human need to converse and communicate to such a granular degree. The way it saw it, the bond they shared was already so immense and powerful – what more did James need?

I'd rather not say.

"Seriously?" James rolled over in the bed and scowled. "How can we move forward if you won't even tell me basic things about yourself? Like, are you a guy, a girl, old, or young? Just basic things like that are all I'm asking."

Uhm, I don't really have a gender per say but I suppose you can refer to me as a he...as for my age I don't really know. I stopped keeping track after the first thousand years or so. Are you satisfied now?

James shook his head no, "I mean, it's something but it's not enough to build a foundation of trust."

Kazav let out a laugh. *Trust is sort of irrelevant at this point, James. We share the closest kind of relationship two beings can have. We need each other to survive, and you feel like you can't trust me?*

"I don't know what to tell you, Kazav. I feel like I need to know more about you before making such a big decision. Would you be fine not knowing a person who held your life in their hands?"

Kazav laughed again. It felt James still didn't seem to understand the point it was trying to make. *I could manage, but then again, I'm not as simple as you are. Besides, anyone can lie about who they are. Knowing that, how could you believe anything I tell you anyway? No, you're just going to have to learn how to trust me regardless.*

That didn't sit right with James. Something inside him snapped. "Listen up, Kazav," he asserted into the dusty, stale air. "You have insulted and belittled me ever since we met. This is supposed to be a partnership, so if you want me to trust you, then you had better give me a reason!"

James sat on the bed and anxiously shook his leg up and down. Memories of yelling and fighting with his family crept into his brain, and he couldn't help but feel shortchanged by all the people he had put his trust in over the years. All of them abandoned him when the going got tough, something he wasn't looking to have to happen again.

Eventually, Kazav broke the stalemate. *Fine,* it mumbled in a defeated tone. *If it would mean that much to you, then I give in. Now, lay back in the bed and close your eyes.*

"Uh, why?"

Just do it, kid,

James rolled his eyes. "Fine, whatever it takes to get the ball rolling."

The moment his head hit the pillow, his body went numb, just like when they first met.

"Um, Kazav? What are you doing?"

He let out a sinister snicker. *Get ready, kid, you're about to go on the ride of your life!*

Fear gripped his body as a feeling of detachment clamped around his skull. It felt like his brain was being torn and sent shooting into the sky.

What happened next was unlike anything James had ever experienced. Images flashed through his mind as his consciousness was sent flying away from the planet and out into the galaxy. Stars zoomed by at lightspeed, and nebulas crashed and swirled into one another as James looked on in awe-inspiring terror.

What felt like an eternity dragged by, and James' mind felt like it was about to explode. His blood was on fire, his heart was pounding, every sense was screaming at him in pain.

"Please, please make this stop!"

Kazav laughed like a madman and shouted, *Don't worry, we're almost there!*

Just as it felt like his heart would explode and his blood would eat through his veins, the journey slowed. James sat in the bed still frozen in place and covered in sweat. He took heavy breaths in and out as he tried to reorient himself.

Kazav was showing James what looked like a movie that was playing in his mind, a vision of sorts. Slowly, a black, almost fluid-looking planet came into view. Small islands of obsidian and volcanic rock rose from the surface of the murky, lifeless waters.

"What is this place?" James asked in between labored breaths.

Letting out a long, disquieting sigh, Kazav said, *"This...is my home."*

James looked on in disbelief as it didn't seem like anything could live on a rock like this. There were no forests, no oceans, and no lifeforms of any kind.

Kazav could tell what James was thinking and remarked, *"It doesn't look like much, but that's because it isn't.*

He pulled James in closer so he could view the

planet's surface. A swirling mass of dark, oily fluid was flowing around the isolated islands that were peppered throughout the world.

James looked on with curiosity. "What's with the dark goo?"

Kazav brought him even closer to the surface until they reached one of the islands. It was a jagged, lonely rock stationed in the middle of the ebony waters. Large crystals jutted out of the center and fissures full of sulfur and brimstone crawled across the entirety of the ground. From the surrounding ocean, two dark, formless beings jumped out of the writhing mass and started walking upright on the ground. They took on a humanoid appearance as they strutted to the middle of the island. Stopping once they got close to another figure, who was chained to the ground, they crossed their arms in contempt and began to let out indiscernible mumbles and groans.

"The figure on the ground is me," Kazav informed. *"The two other figures walking over are judges."*

They exchanged more aggressive and irritated grumbling sounds before Kazav realized James couldn't understand.

"Sorry! I'll translate this for you."

"Do you have anything to say for yourself?" one of the beings shouted to Kazav. "Anything at all to justify your heinous activity?"

Kazav looked up at the judges and snidely replied, "Only this: you claim we should never get involved in the lives of other beings, but do you have any idea how lost they are, how much they need our help? I would rather spend eternity chained to this rock than refuse to assist those miserable wretches."

"That's good," the other judge interjected. "Because that's exactly what you'll be doing for the rest of time."

They drew out more beaming chains and threw them at Kazav, pinning him to one of the crystals poking from the ground, preventing any kind of mobility whatsoever.

The world Kazav was showing James began to blur out of existence. After the vision ended, feeling came rushing back into James' body, and the room he was in shifted back into focus.

"Wow! What was all that?"

Kazav responded in a labored voice, *"That was what you wanted from me, right? To see where I came from and stuff like that?"*

"Well, yeah, but I have so many questions! Why were you cuffed to the ground? How did you get away? What are you made of exactly?"

Kazav cut him off before he could continue: *"Look, kid, that whole experience made me kinda tired. I promise I'll show you more another time, but for now, let's focus on what our next move will be."*

James nodded and took a deep breath. "Good point. We still have a decision to make."

7/WELCOME TO
THE GUILD

James left the room and headed out to the main hall. As he walked through the metal doors, the entire table of heroes turned to face him, eager to hear what his choice would be. He looked at each of them briefly and then at Sparrow, who raised an eyebrow out of tense anticipation.

"What's it gonna be?" she asked.

James paused for effect and, after finalizing the choice in his heart, replied, "I'm in."

The table of heroes cheered and clapped with excitement, making James feel both flattered and uncomfortable. All the attention was on him – something he had never really experienced before.

Sparrow walked over to him and slapped him on the back. "Welcome to the team!"

He winced as she struck him. "Thanks. What happens now?"

"The first thing we need to get you is a proper hero uniform. You can't claim to belong to the Heroes Guild if you don't have the right attire."

James looked around at the others' costumes and asked, "Do I have any creative control?"

"Yes, but we can make one for you if you prefer to be surprised. I personally think you would look good in black and red."

"In that case, why don't you surprise me?"

She gave him a wink and playfully punched his shoulder.

After walking back over to her seat, she clicked a button that was built into the armrest and spoke into an intercom. "Bella, we have another suit job for you."

Not a moment later, a disheveled, crazy-haired, and manic-looking woman in a white lab coat burst into the room and started taking James' measurements.

Sparrow giggled as James got wrapped in measuring tape. "This is Bella. She's our resident genius slash mad scientist."

"Nice to meet you," he remarked as the woman got a little too close for comfort.

Bella apologized for being so invasive. "Sorry. I must get as accurate a measurement as possible or the suit will squeeze some...sensitive areas."

As quick as she burst in, she burst back out, zipping away, and disappearing behind the steel doors leading to her lab. With the general introductions out of the way, Sparrow took James to his living quarters. Heading out a different exit, she led him through a nicer, more active section of the guildhall until coming to a stop in front of a doorway.

"This will be your room," she informed as she pointed inside.

He was delighted to see that it was rather comfy. The bed looked soft and inviting; the furniture was modern and in one piece. There was even a steamer chest he could use to store his equipment. Bookshelves lined the back wall, giving the room a scholarly touch as well as filling the air with scents of leather and decaying parchment.

She noticed he had his eyes fixed on the library and motioned for him to browse. "The books are training manuals full of tricks, tips, and insights for how to use your powers effectively. I recommend you read them whenever you get a chance."

James flipped through one of the old volumes until something caught his eye. Towards the back of the book was an entire section on the hero Quasar. The image that was displayed next to his name reminded James of the card he had at home. "Do I live here now, or can I still go back to my apartment?"

Sparrow thought about it and said, "I wouldn't recommend it. This is a more secure option for you. Once word gets out you're a hero, every monster and mobster for miles around is going to have you on their radar."

"Wow, I didn't even think about that. I suppose there is more to being a hero than running around in tights and zapping monsters with lasers, isn't there?"

She giggled and said, "Well, it's ninety-nine percent trying not to die and one percent fighting monsters in tights."

"Ah, well at least we still get that one percent!"

Sparrow rolled her eyes and let out a snicker. "I see you are a jokester. That's good because this life can beat you up. It's good to keep things light. What's not a joke is how bad you smell."

James looked over his clothes and winced. His hoodie was covered in sewer grime, and his jeans were tattered and caked with mysterious fluids. "Good point," he grumbled.

"There are some clean clothes you can use in your room. Why don't you clean up a bit, and then I will give you a tour of the building?" Sparrow gave him some privacy as he changed.

Once he took off his old clothes, he was half tempted to toss them in the fireplace. From the steamer trunk, he found a monotone set of clothes that were a bit baggy on him.

"You look like a male nurse," she teased as he walked into the hallway.

James let out a comical huff. "Thanks, I will take it as a compliment."

"Whatever makes you feel better. Now, follow me."

They walked down the hallway until they reached the door to Bella's lab. Electronic devices beeped and flashed as bubbling cylinders full of glowing liquids filled and emptied throughout a never-ending array of vials and flasks. It reminded James of the *Frankenstein* movies he used to watch.

"This is the lab," Sparrow announced as she spun Bella around in her chair. "This is where we can request gadgets, supplies, and experiment with objects and substances we find in the field. If you ever need anything, then Bella is the girl to talk to."

Sparrow continued the tour by showing him the dining hall. It was decorated top to bottom with ancient hero relics and odd, sometimes disturbing-looking trophies. Posters and paintings hung on the walls, leaving virtually no space untouched.

James poked one of the stuffed monster heads, shuddering as he investigated its beady, lifeless eyes. "You must work up quite the appetite. I hope this guy wasn't one of your meals, or I may consider eating out more often."

"Speaking of food, we have a full, modern kitchen that is restocked frequently. We don't have a cook, so if you do want to eat something specific, you're gonna have to take the initiative and make it yourself."

She led him through the door to the kitchen at the other end of the dining hall. It was full of high-tech cooking equipment and food preservation cases. Shiny knives were lined up on top of the counters, and every sort of cooking utensil imaginable was hanging from hooks under a cooking hood. From the kitchen, they walked down another hallway until they entered a room full of gaming equipment and relaxation stations.

"This is our entertainment room. You can come here anytime to unwind and relax. Just don't leave it a mess, or you won't be allowed back in."

James looked around and let out an impressed whistle. Sparrow whistled back a playful tune and waved him over.

"Last but not least, I'm going to show the biggest, and perhaps most important room in the entire building."

Once they arrived James understood what she meant. Workout equipment, training courses, VR systems, and a giant pool were just some of the features that made up the gargantuan arena.

"This is our training facility!" Sparrow announced with fanfare. "We meet in here every morning to hone our skills and learn to fight as a team. Your first day will be tomorrow, so make sure you get a good night's sleep because we get up before sunrise."

James gave her a perturbed look. "That sounds really early."

"It's not so bad once you get used to it," she reassured. "One last thing before I let you go. Follow me back to the main hall so I can administer you the hero's oath. All who take this oath are sworn to put aside their own interests and vow to serve the city with all their heart."

Kazav snickered sarcastically. *"Hero's oath? Oh*

yeah, that will stop people from abusing their power. Why don't you ask them to pinky promise while you're at it?"

"Shut it!" James hissed aloud.

Sparrow looked back at him, a sneer forming on her face. "Excuse me?"

James forgot that nobody else could hear Kazav and tried to apologize. "Sorry! I was just saying shut it, like shut it, girl, I can't wait to be a hero, haha..."

She turned around without a reply, leaving James to wallow in embarrassment. Now back in the main hall, Sparrow had James face her and instructed him to repeat everything she was about to say. "I, James, promise to serve and protect my city with courage and valor. To put the safety of its citizens above all else, and to be willing to risk my life for their well-being."

Once he finished repeating the oath, the room let out a boisterous cheer. Owl popped open a bottle and poured him a glass of champagne.

As he took a sip, Hawk walked over and punched his shoulder. "You're a hero now, James, don't let us down."

Each of the other team members came up and congratulated him, welcoming him to his new life. Hours flew by as each of them regaled the room with stories of their early days as a hero. Before anyone realized it, the clock was chiming its midnight tune.

Sparrow broke up the fun and guided James back to his room. "Try to get some rest. You're going to be working pretty hard tomorrow because when we train, we really train."

He put his hand out, gesturing for her to shake it. She looked down at it and hesitantly complied.

"What was that all about?" she asked.

"I just wanted to thank you. I didn't know what to do, so I gave you a handshake."

"Ah, you're welcome. I'm glad to have you on board. Now seriously, get some sleep."

He tried to go to bed, he really did, but the excitement over this new chapter in his life was too hard to fight. He lay awake until he was jolted by the sound of Sparrow banging on his door.

"Rise and shine!" she howled from the other side. "Oh, and by the way, there is a surprise for you outside the door!"

James jumped up and peered outside. Resting against the wall was a mannequin outfitted in a super suit. A note attached to the collar read, *For James. From Bella. Try not to get it dirtied on the first day.*

He strapped in and checked himself out in the mirror. "Nice," he muttered as he flexed and posed. It was a dark, durable fabric that was designed to take a beating. The primary color was black, but the bendable sections in the sleeves and legs were a dark crimson. He felt it looked like a mix between a biker outfit and riot gear. Flapping his cape, he darted through the room, looking back to watch it flutter in the air.

Sparrow knocked on the door and asked if she

could come in. He gave her permission to enter, and she strutted inside. "Well, well, well, don't we look dashing in a costume?"

James blushed at the compliment. "Yeah, Bella did an amazing job! It fits like a glove."

Sparrow gave him a thumbs up and said, "I just came by to make sure you were ready for your first day of training."

"Right! So, what's that going to involve?"

"Well, the first thing we do is go through a series of basic tests similar to what we administer to people getting examined for superhuman abilities."

As they walked over to the training hall, James struggled to fight back a wave of resentment now building in his gut. He remembered taking that test a long time ago when his brother's powers first manifested.

After they finished with the formalities, Sparrow motioned for James to enter a chalk circle drawn on the floor.

"What's all this about?" he asked suspiciously.

Sparrow pointed at a long metal cylinder and shouted, "You see that tube in front of you? That tube is going to launch projectiles of varying speeds and densities at you in order to test your reflexes and durability."

Before James could object, a metal ball came flying out and struck him in the chest. He fell to the floor huffing and wheezing as took in the shock of what just happened. After a few seconds, Sparrow motioned for him to get back in the circle for another round.

"Seriously?" he cried out.

"Seriously! Now get a move on! We've got a lot to do today!"

Shot after shot came out at him until, after getting bruised and beaten, he started to deflect them with some degree of consistency.

Sparrow walked out from behind the safety glass and said, "Okay, that's enough for one day. Let's move on to the offensive portion of your test."

Now at the next station, Sparrow began to explain how it worked. "This machine is designed to be struck and will give back a precise reading of your raw physical strength. Now, give it everything you got," she ordered while pointing at the target painted on the side.

James wound up his fist and smacked the testing pad. The machine let out a ding and displayed a number on the screen above.

"Five thousand PSI," James read off the computer. "Is that good?"

Sparrow made a so-so motion with her hand. "Well, the average professional boxer's PSI tops out at about seven hundred. Yours is more than five times that number. It's not bad, but it can be greatly improved."

Walking over to the machine, she struck it casually. The force of her punch let out a crack into the air and sent the number up to nine thousand.

She strutted and stated, "Once you get to that level, I'll be impressed."

The rest of the day was like an Olympic event. Running track, hurdles, swimming laps. James half expected there to be an awards ceremony at the finish line.

Now done with the last course of the day, Sparrow said the four words James had longed to hear: "You ready to eat?"

"Everything. I am ready to eat everything"

She giggled and wrapped his arm around her, supporting him as they joined the rest of the team in the dining hall.

"So, you gonna stick around?" Hawk asked James through a mouthful of mashed potatoes. "Or did the training kick your butt too hard?"

Falcon smacked his cheek, causing Hawk to spit all over the table. "Lay off 'em. He took those cannon shots like a champ!"

James chuckled as he rubbed the bruised sections of his body. "It will take a lot more than that to get rid of me."

The team laughed at his quip before ripping into the meal. Mashed potatoes, meatloaf, turkey, assorted vegetables, it was a full-on buffet.

Now relaxing in the entertainment room, the team shared stories about their own first day of training. They laughed, they teased, they fought – it was a camaraderie James had never known before. For the first time in his life, he started to feel like he belonged somewhere, like his life was starting to make sense.

8/SOLO MISSION

Training and studying, training and studying – this was all James knew for the next three months. Impressed with his progress, Sparrow called a team meeting to discuss the next step in James' career.

"Thank you for meeting together a bit earlier than usual," she started. "As you can see, James is the only one missing from this briefing. That's because he is the subject of this conversation. I think it's clear to all that James has made some astounding progress in the short time he has been with us."

The team whispered among themselves, all in agreement.

"The kid's crazy durable," Falcon exclaimed. "I saw him get shot in the face and spit the bullets out on the ground!"

"Pshh, that never happened!" Hawk shouted. "Stop making up stories to try and sound cool."

"I ain't lying! I saw it happen with my own eyes!"

Sparrow took a bullhorn and blasted the siren until all attention was back on her. "Hawk and Falcon...can we have one meeting that doesn't get derailed by your pointless nonsense?"

"Safe money is on no," Falcon frankly admitted.

She rolled her eyes and picked up where she left off. "While I have my concerns with the speed his powers are developing, I have seen nothing less than a dedicated, devoted team member when we bring him along on field missions. That's why I think we should let him tackle his first solo assignment."

"A capital idea," Owl stated. "He has more than demonstrated all the fundamentals of what being a hero is all about. Plus, he got me this bird figurine!" Owl took the toy out from his pocket and began to play with it, making it hop along the surface of the table.

Static sat up in her chair and agreed. "While he may be a little strange, talking to himself at random moments and whatnot, Owl is right. I say we let him handle a solo op."

"So, are we all in agreement?" Sparrow asked as she looked around the room. Everyone nodded yes. "Perfect! I'll grab James, and we can tell him the good news!"

A short while later, Sparrow returned with James in tow. He took his seat, and the meeting started.

"Lots to talk about today," she announced. "For one, crime is down, while monster attacks continue to rise, so I want everyone's focus to shift toward that." Now walking back and forth across the room, she added, "Secondly, we need to talk about a new concern in our precinct."

She pulled out an edict from the Heroes Guild HQ and read it aloud: "It has come to our attention that a new anti-hero sect has been reported in your guild's patrol radius. It is recommended that you dispatch a hero with the task of tracking down and investigating this potential threat."

Sparrow looked over to James. "I think this is a mission you could handle on your own."

The anxiety at the thought of his first solo mission made his throat tighten. "Really?"

Sparrow nodded. "Yup, we all think it's time. This is a low-pressure mission that will get you more familiar with the city and give you the chance to break in your new skills."

Everyone clapped for him as Sparrow plopped the instructions on the desk.

"Wow, this is huge!" James said as he shook his leg like a madman.

She could tell he was getting tense and offered some reassurance. "Hey, you got this. Just do your best, and I promise you won't let us down."

He slowed his leg and gave her a smile. "Thanks, Sparrow, I'll do my best."

"One more thing," she added. "Have you come up with a hero name like we talked about? Remember: this is how everyone will know and identify you, so make sure it's one you like."

After a lot of back and forth with Kazav, they

had indeed settled on a hero name they both liked. Looking out at the table he announced, "My hero name is going to be Night Phoenix."

Sparrow and the team clapped in support of his choice. "Well then, welcome, Night Phoenix, the name certainly suits you. Now get out there and gather all the information you can on this new group."

"Yes, ma'am!" he replied gleefully.

After gearing up and reading through the file, he took off into the city. It had been reported that people matching the description were spotted around the southern end of their guild's territory. Witnesses reported a group of strange people going in and out of an abandoned building several miles south of his current position.

As he leapt from rooftop to rooftop, he couldn't help but feel amused. Just a few months ago, he would never have dreamed of being able to cover so much ground in such little time. In the past, a journey of several miles used to be an ordeal but was now just a few leaps and bounds away.

While flying between buildings, he looked down at the people below. Some of them would point in awe when they spotted him. Others would clap and cheer or even ask for photos and autographs if they could catch him in time. One thing James learned fast was that there were a lot of people who didn't like heroes. That didn't surprise him, as he had agreed until recently.

Eventually, he got to the general area the file

had mentioned. He decided to use one of the taller buildings for a vantage point and started a wall jump to get to the top. It was hard work avoiding the windows when jumping off the sides, and he broke more than a few in training before he got the feel for it. With a swift final kick off the side of the wall, he reached the top and perched himself over the edge. Like a stoic gargoyle, he leaned over the city with a motionless gaze.

The building he was looking for was a rundown factory near the edge of town. The report didn't name a specific street number, so he would have to do some recon if he was to find out which one to inspect.

"Let me know if you see something interesting, Kazav."

"Yes, sir," he playfully replied. *"I must say, I like this new, confident James."*

Several hours had gone by of scanning and patrolling the area before James saw anything noteworthy. As he looked out over to the edge of the city, he noticed several suspicious-looking vehicles shuttling back and forth. The people coming in and out of the vehicles were all dressed and looked the same and greeted each other with odd hand gestures. Black cloaks covered their faces and long, dark robes hid the rest of their bodies.

Kazav let out a hearty laugh. *"I'd say that warrants a closer look. It's almost like they want people to know they're up to something."*

James jumped off the edge of the building and entered a freefall. Hitting the concrete ceiling of the building below, he made his way across several other rooftops before reaching the outskirts of the city.

Hiding behind a clock tower, he watched as a large group of people exited the vans and filed into the factory across from him. He hung back until all of them were out of sight, and then jumped down to inspect the vans. They were all empty, except for a few bags that had a strange insignia. It was of a red orb being held in a withered old hand.

"Spooky," he mused as he snapped a picture with his phone. Now moving on to the building, he walked around the side, hoping to find a secondary access point. Jumping through a broken window, James made his entry.

The factory looked long abandoned. Old equipment lay in piles on the floor, collecting dust and giving shelter to an endless variety of creepy crawlers. He stepped over the dilapidated gear as he searched for clues as to where the group might have gone off to. All the rooms were empty, and the only sounds he could pick up were of mice and birds darting throughout the facility. A normal person might have given up, but James, with his new and sensitive eyesight, could see vague friction marks on the ground ahead.

As he leaned in to inspect the wall, a light breeze brushed against his cheek. A closer look revealed an expertly hidden secret door built into the wall.

"Very clever," James remarked as he felt around, trying to find the way in. After searching the length of the wall, he discovered a fuse box that didn't seem to connect to anything. James pulled the lever down and heard a click. Moments later, the wall parted, revealing a long stone stairwell leading underground.

Every instinct was telling him not to go down there. In every scary movie he had ever seen, entering a secret doorway was a sure way to wind up dead. James shook his head and steeled his nerves for whatever he might find on the other side. No matter how spooky things got, he was not about to fail this mission.

The second he passed through the doorway, it slammed shut behind him, leaving him with only one option: to press on. The stairwell was made of old stone and covered in strange etchings. Freshly lit candles lined the walls and illuminated the carved statues of strange creatures placed throughout.

He reached the bottom of the stairwell and could detect the faint echoes of someone shouting into the crypt. James crept closer until he came upon a very strange scene. The group that had entered the ruins sat around in a half-circle while a man in a cloak gave a passionate and rousing speech.

"Our long wait is almost over!" the man shouted in a guttural tone. Cheers and clapping thundered into the hall as the observers engaged with the speaker. "We will no longer suffer under the noxious influence of the so-called *heroes* of this rotting world!"

The hooded figure jumped off the slab of stone he was standing on and, reaching into a satchel, pulled out a mysterious dark crystal. He held it up into the air for everyone to see as he continued his ranting. "What I hold in my hands is the solution to our long-awaited cry for freedom! With the power of these crystals, we can raise an army to aid in our fight to cleanse this planet."

As James looked at the crystal, an overwhelming urge to reach out and touch it gripped him. It was as though there was a magnetic force compelling him to get closer. The feeling passed once the man put it back in his pack and out of sight. James let out a gasp of relief and rubbed his eyes to get his focus back.

Now back on the slab, the stranger continued to shout to the crowd. "Our leader is already among us just waiting for the opportune moment to bring the heroes of this world to their knees and take that which rightfully belongs to him!"

The crowd shouted manically in agreement and jumped around in their seats. James shook his head in disbelief. He couldn't understand why anyone would want to get involved in something like this. He wondered just what it was they thought they were going to accomplish.

"In one year, this world and all who inhabit it will finally get the leader it deserves and will be forced to submit to his fear-inspiring power!" The figure pointed to a massive stone carving behind him. It was of a boney, wretched, and vile-looking creature clutching a sphere in its hands.

Kazav snickered as he listened to the man shout and strut for the crowd. *"Well, well, looks like creeps and weirdos exist on every planet I visit. I was hoping this one would be different, but maybe that was asking for too much."*

James nodded in agreement. "Yeah, there are weirdos everywhere you go. Haven't you ever been inside a superstore?"

They shared a brief chuckle and then went back to spying. It looked as though the cult leader was wrapping up his speech.

"For now, my children, we will disperse back into our mundane lives and wait eagerly for his arrival. In just one year's time, the Nexus Orb will no longer be out of our reach, and with it, this world will be reborn!"

The crowd cried out in loud and cheerful joy as they rose from their seats. Then, following the leader, the members began to file up the staircase where James was eavesdropping.

Kazav panicked. *"Kid, we gotta go! They're heading right back toward you!"*

James let out a muffled groan and took off running until he got to the top of the staircase.

"Hurry up and open the door!" Kazav demanded.

"I'm trying! I can't find a switch on this side!" James frantically replied. Feeling like he had no other option, he kicked the door down, sending it flying off the wall.

The sound of metal crashing into concrete alerted the cultists to his presence. "What in the world was that? Who's there?" a voice called out from below.

James didn't wait around so they could find out. He dashed outside through another broken window and made his way back to the guildhall at breakneck speed.

"So much for an easy first mission," Kazav teased.

9/THE INVITATION

James reported everything he uncovered the second he got back to the guildhall. Sparrow and the team hung on every word, their faces growing more concerned with each passing second. Once he finished relating the details of his mission, Sparrow walked to her chair and shouted over the intercom for Bella.

In the woman burst, like a manic, overly caffeinated chipmunk. Papers full of charts and graphs seemed to flutter behind her everywhere she went.

"Show her," Sparrow commanded James while pointing to Bella.

He reached his hand out so she could see but rather than look at what he had pulled up on the screen, she snatched the device out of his hand and uploaded its contents to her computer. Images flashed by and a percentile match bar popped up below, giving comparison estimates for each picture. It stopped on an image that was labeled as a one-hundred-percent match, and she displayed the accompanying picture beside it on the screen.

Bella nodded as her suspicion was confirmed. "This image is of a stone relief carved thousands of years ago. It was found inside an ancient hero's burial tomb by an HQ-funded excavation team."

Sparrow ran her hands through her hair and let out a heavy breath. "This means your hunch was correct, doesn't it?"

Bella swallowed a knot in her throat and adjusted her lab coat. "Yes, unfortunately, I was right."

James grabbed his phone and shoved it in his pocket. "What's going on here?" he asked while looking back and forth at Sparrow and Bella. "It sounds really bad."

Sparrow tapped her finger on the table and stared off into space. Everyone knew not to bother her when she got like that. Interrupting her train of thought was a surefire way of getting chewed out.

She broke the silence with a bold announcement: "Everyone, out. I'm contacting HQ about this."

"Seriously?" Falcon cried out. "Is it that bad of a situation that you feel you need to bother HQ?"

Sparrow turned her head to face him and gave him a look so intense it could burn a hole through an iron plate.

"Never mind," he whimpered as he scurried out the door. The rest of the team followed suit and made their way to the exit. James was almost through the door when Sparrow snapped her fingers at him. "Not you, James, you stay."

Owl teased him as he walked out the door, "I wouldn't wanna be you right now."

James walked over to Sparrow as she furiously typed into her keyboard, mouthing the words she was spelling silently.

"Something wrong?" he asked in hopes that she wasn't about to end him.

She shook her head and held her finger up, indicating she needed a moment. Once she was done typing, she put him at ease. "I just need you here in case HQ has any questions they want to ask you directly."

She smiled as she stood up and adjusted the collar of his suit. "You should count yourself lucky. Very few heroes have the privilege of talking face to face with a high-ranking official of the Heroes' Guild."

The terminal dinged, and a massive blue screen materialized in the air. A man in a grey suit entered the field of view. With a head full of white hair and a face covered in wrinkles, James could almost see the stress and experience exuding off him.

"Afternoon, Official Franklin," Sparrow greeted as she stood up to salute him.

"A good afternoon to you, Shadow Sparrow," Franklin returned. "I trust you have an urgent matter to discuss for you to be contacting me on such short notice."

She shook her leg wildly as she sat in her chair. James had never seen her so nervous when talking to another person. "Apologies for requesting this meeting so suddenly, but I felt this couldn't afford to wait."

"I see," Franklin replied, his face scrunching into

a troubled scowl. "Very well. Brief me on the situation."

"I'm afraid it has to do with the Nexus Orb."

Franklin's face turned pale as he looked on at the images on the screen. "Oh my, that is a serious issue indeed." His aged voice cracked as he spoke.

Sparrow motioned for James to come into view. He moved into position next to Sparrow, unsure of what to do next. Then she introduced him. "This is Night Phoenix. He was the hero who investigated the anti-hero meeting that HQ instructed us to investigate. He has information that you will want to hear."

Franklin gave James a nod and said, "Proceed, young hero."

James went through the details he uncovered. The symbols, the crystal, the giant stone carvings – he left nothing out. By the end of his report, Franklin was nearly falling out of his chair from anxiety. After staring off into space, his mind racing from the shock, Franklin typed something into his computer. A message popped up in Sparrow's inbox from Franklin, and as she read the subject line, her jaw dropped.

"I sent you and James an invitation to HQ. I want you both here to brief the entire Council about your findings."

Sparrow's legs turned to rubber. "The...the Council?"

"Indeed. First thing tomorrow morning, I want you both here with a full written report. The email

I sent has your security clearance and meeting information. Don't be late." Franklin gave a salute and signed off. The blue screen disappeared, leaving a confused James and a starstruck Sparrow alone.

"So, that sounds big," James remarked, almost as a question.

She looked at him with her eyes as wide as they could be. "It's incredible!" she exclaimed. "I have been a hero for over ten years, and I have never gotten an invitation to HQ. This is unbelievable!"

She started her report immediately, completely forgetting that James was right behind her, watching as she compiled everything into a folder.

"What's the Nexus Orb?" James asked as she put an image of it in a subfolder.

"Ah!" she screeched. "Oh, James, you scared me. I completely forgot you were here." She laughed and turned around in her chair. "What was the question?"

"What is the Nexus Orb? It sounds important."

Sparrow hesitated. She wasn't sure she should be sharing information on such a powerful relic. "You know what? You're going to find out about it from my report, so I may as well just tell you now." She motioned for him to sit down and asked, "Have you ever heard of the Nexus Orb before today?"

James shook his head and told her no.

"Figures. The Heroes Guild has been doing everything it can since the Orb was first discovered to make sure it never falls into the wrong hands. That includes keeping it a secret from the world."

"Okay, but what exactly is the Orb's significance?"

Sparrow smirked as she closed the screen, giving him her full attention. "Do you know what gives us our powers?" she asked pointedly.

"Huh. I've never really asked myself that question. I always thought it was a genetic thing."

"It's the Nexus Orb!" Sparrow exclaimed. "How it got here, we don't know, and who could have made it is still up for debate, but what we do know is that when it arrived on our planet, people started gaining extraordinary abilities. Every superhero, supervillain, and monster that has ever existed owes its power to the Orb.

"So where is it?" James asked excitedly.

"That is not something I would know. Only the highest-ranking heroes have access to that information, and they are forbidden from sharing it with anyone. Even just asking about it can get you expelled from the Guild."

She turned to face her computer and went back to her report.

He was about to ask more questions, but she raised a finger and hushed him. "I'm sorry, James, but I have a lot of work to do before we meet with HQ tomorrow. How about you go freshen up so you smell nice for the meeting? Also, when was the last time you shaved?"

James ran his fingers through his scruffy-looking stubble and gave himself a sniff. "Wow, good point, maybe a shower would be in order."

"Yeah, yeah, you do that, and make sure you're all set for the big meeting. You and I are going to be one of a handful of heroes to ever stand before the entire Council! The last thing you want to be worried about is his having stinky pit smell."

James walked out and left Sparrow to her report, looking himself over on his way back to his room. "Hey, Kazav, what do you make of all this?"

"I've seen a lot of cultists, zealots, and weirdos in my time, kid, and they all have one thing in common: they're all nuts!"

James let out a gut-busting laugh. "What about this Orb? Have you ever heard of something like that?"

"Our kind doesn't interfere with other worlds. It's part of why I am in so much trouble with the judges. But if I think long and hard, it does ring a bell. Yours isn't the only planet with heroes, so it may be that there are more than one of these strange Orbs."

"Well, I suppose it's nothing to get worked up about. Sparrow has a lot on her mind as it is. I don't need to be adding to her plate with an endless list of questions."

After a long, hot shower and a clean shave, James got everything ready for the next day.

As he lay in bed, trying to fall asleep, Kazav roused him with a manic screech. *"James!"* *he shrieked.*

"Something doesn't feel right, kid! I feel this dark force looming over us."

James rubbed his head as he recovered from the shrillness of Kazav's meltdown. "What kind of force?"

"I'm not sure, but it feels hostile. Maybe we should go outside and check it out?"

James closed his eyes and attempted to ignore him. With Sparrow's ability to hide the guildhall's location, he saw no need to panic. Kazav responded to his apathy by sending a spasm through his body, forcing him onto the floor.

"What was that for?"

"You wouldn't get up, so I got creative."

Now fully alert, James said, "Fine. What is it you want me to do?"

"Just head outside and make sure everything is on the level."

James suited up and snuck outside via the secondary entrance, a secret hatch that led to the fields above.

Pale moonlight beamed down, illuminating the field of flowering grasses that hid the hatch from sight. It would have been a beautiful moment if not for the impending sense of doom James was getting from Kazav.

He looked out at the field and scanned the horizon. Nothing was in sight, just a few wild animals roaming about in the night.

"I don't see anything," James whispered with an

attitude.

"Just keep looking. Maybe walk around a bit. I won't feel better until I'm sure nothing is out here."

James was amused by his paranoia. It was not at all like Kazav to express concern or fear. He almost had the impulse to tease him.

"So, uh, Kazav, what do you think is after us – that raccoon, or maybe that opossum?"

"Just be quiet and keep looking," Kazav shot back.

After twenty minutes of searching in the damp and musty woods, James decided to call it quits.

"Look, Kazav there's nothing out there. Are you sure you're not just a bit nervous about this whole meeting at HQ? Because I am and-"

Before he could finish his sentence, a flash of light streaked across the sky, slamming into the ground, sending James flying backward as flames engulfed the ground. Stepping out of the inferno was a person he would never have expected to see in a million years.

With a chiseled jaw and a tight, sinuous body, the man walked towards him, full of confidence and authority. James sat frozen on the ground as he tried to think of what to say.

"Jeremy, is that you? How did you... Where did you..." James stammered as he tried to form the words to put to his feelings.

His brother closed the gap and reached down with his hand in an offer to help him up off the ground. With a deep and powerful voice, Jeremy said, "Hello, brother, long time no see." Jeremy then glanced down at his hand, which was still outstretched. "Are you going to take it, or do you feel more comfortable on the ground?"

James got up on his own and wiped the dirt off his suit in a display of independence. His brother pulled his hand back and let it rest. Jeremy wasn't surprised by the lack of brotherly affection. There was a lot of bad blood between them, and he knew it.

"It's good to see you again, little bro."

The statement made James' face twitch. "That's an odd thing to say considering you haven't seen me in over ten years."

"Are you still bitter about how things ended with us? Why can't you mature and move on? It won't do you any good clinging to the past."

The mood quickly devolved as they both vented their frustrations. After a back and forth of barbed comments and accusations, Jeremy cut the conversation short. "You know what? I'm not here to pick old wounds."

James crossed his arms and asked, "Well then, why are you here?"

As Jeremy moved forward, his muscles bulged from underneath his suit, and his cape flapped in the wind. "I could be asking you the same question. There I am back at HQ when I get a summons to appear before the Council for a briefing. I look at who the speakers will be, and guess the face I see on the report?" He pointed at James and asked, "You want to explain to me why you're fooling around in the Heroes' Guild when you're not even a hero?"

James' blood boiled as Jeremy derided him. This argument brought up a lot of unresolved feelings, and James was no longer interested in staying silent. With his newfound powers giving him the confidence to speak, he replied, "I too am a hero, and if you need proof, I would be happy to provide it."

Kazav decided now would be a good time to chime in. *"Woah, kid, calm down. I don't like your jerk of a brother any more than you do, but I don't think picking a fight with him is a good idea."*

He ignored Kazav's warning and took a battle stance.

"Fine!" Jeremy shouted. "You want to play hero? Show me what you've got."

James tensed up. He could feel Kazav trying to restrain him. *"Look, James, you're not even close to the same level as him. If he decides to fight you, then it's not going to end well. Please just try to calm down!"*

Kazav's pleas started to sink in, and James took a few deep breaths. He regained his composure and realized it wasn't worth giving his brother the satisfaction. He did, however, have a few closing thoughts to share. "Jeremy, I don't need to prove anything. I am a hero, and you know what? I'm going to be more of a hero than you could ever dream of being!"

Jeremy was taken aback by the newfound confidence in his little brother. But brother or not, a challenge had been issued to his ego, and he was not about to let that go. "Fine," he coldly replied. "I'll make you prove it."

Jeremy raised his foot into the air and slammed it down on the ground, causing huge chunks of rock to burst up from beneath the dirt. He smacked them towards James and shouted, "A real hero should have no trouble dealing with this!"

James prepared himself for the wall of gravel and granite that was flying to meet him. With his fist at the ready, he slammed into the largest of the chunks and split it apart, causing rubble and debris to shoot out in all directions.

The dust settled, and Jeremy watched on in shock as James stood there unharmed. "But you failed all the tests. How is this possible?"

James shrugged. "Maybe I was just a late bloomer?

Jeremy flew until he and James were face to face. He then issued a warning: "I will be keeping a close eye on you from here on out and let me assure you that if your newfound power is a threat to the Guild in any way, I will take action to protect it."

"I'm sure you will," James poked back sarcastically.

Releasing James' collar, Jeremy took off, tearing up ground as he blasted off like a rocket.

Once he was out of sight, Kazav laid into James. *"Kid, are you nuts? What were you thinking, challenging your brother like that? You're lucky he didn't snap you in two!"*

He brushed off Kazav's concerns. "I knew he wouldn't do anything serious. I called his bluff, is all."

"You got off easy, if you ask me."

"Are you afraid of my brother?" James asked in a mocking tone.

"No, kid, I'm afraid of what he could do to your body, as in, turn it into pulp. Now simmer down and get some sleep. The dread I was feeling is gone now, so hopefully, you won't have any more late-night visitors."

"Gladly," James said through a yawn.

10/HQ

With the morning well underway, James and Sparrow met in the main hall to prep for the briefing. Sparrow had been up most of the night getting every detail of her report looking perfect and, as a result, was looking quite tired.

James walked up from behind and leaned over her chair. "How do we get to HQ?" he asked, causing her to let out a startled gasp.

"Don't scare me like that!" she shouted, smacking his arm in retaliation. Pointing over to a flashing disk, she said, "This is a transport marker. An agent from HQ will lock on to our signal and beam us over when they arrive."

James raised an eyebrow; his interest was piqued. "Beam? As in, teleport?"

She nodded. "Yup, they have agents that they recruit specifically for their ability to teleport. It's the only way to get in and out of HQ, and it's highly regulated."

James felt a prick in his brain. A sense of dread was building in him as spillover from Kazav.

"Kazav, are you okay?" he asked internally so as

not to alarm Sparrow.

"I'm fine, kid, it just feels like we're heading into the belly of the beast is all."

James' eyes narrowed. *"What do you mean?"*

"We are about to enter the most sacred and heavily guarded location on this planet. Most of the people there probably wouldn't respond well if they found out you had basically conned your way into being a hero."

James' heart fluttered at the thought of being discovered. *"Wow, I didn't even think about that. Do you think we should be worried? I mean, is there any way for them to sense that about us?"*

"I don't know, kid, I guess we'll find out soon enough."

Sparrow looked at James and could tell he was nervous. "Hey, you'll be fine," she reassured him. "Besides, if anyone should be nervous, it's me. I'm the one who will be doing most of the talking."

That was more than okay with James; he hated public speaking. There were few things worse in his mind than being in front of a room of judgmental strangers forcing you to speak. They chatted as they sipped coffee, sharing concerns and fears until a bright light erupted in the middle of the room, forcing them to shield their faces.

Once the blinding rays subsided, a man stepped forward. James and Sparrow both raised an eyebrow at his appearance. He was tall, wearing a black leather trench coat and sunglasses. His hair was greased and spiked back with a slight part on the left side.

"I'll be your transport," he announced in a burly tone.

They put their drinks down on the table and walked over to the mysterious stranger. He held out his hands and motioned for them to take hold. James reached out first and gave the hand a firm grip. Sparrow followed suit and gently placed her fingers around his palm. With their hands locked, the man began to glow once more and as his body disappeared, so too did James and Sparrow.

The next thing they saw was the interior of a large metal room they had just materialized in. They were confused. The room looked more like a prison cell than a high-tech headquarters.

"Follow me," the transporter commanded, his tone now serious.

"This is not at all what I was expecting," James remarked to Kazav soundlessly as they scampered up a set of dark, metal stairs.

"Don't worry, kid, I get the feeling we're about to be pleasantly surprised."

Now waiting in front of a large metal blast door, the transporter looked back at them and said, "Make sure to mind your manners and respect the other heroes. They are all on duty and don't have time to chat."

They nodded affirmatively. Satisfied, he typed a password in the keypad, and the doors started to part. Once on the other side, James and Sparrow let out a gasp.

The doors opened into a massive arena that looked like it belonged in a science-fiction movie. A waterfall feature sat near the top of the ceiling and rained a torrent down onto an artificial lake below. The apiary was a magical mix of nature and high-tech design. White, metallic floors sprawled out in all directions, allowing people to walk, bike, and hoverboard to their destination. It was like a whole other world that was guarded away from the outside, a paradise in the middle of a slum. Heroes of all stripes and districts roamed as they interacted with an endless army of lab techs, officials, and sidekicks.

Some of the heroes were big names that James recognized from his card collection. Thunderclap, Cosmic Ray, Black Dragon. He was surprised to see them all in one place and all in the flesh.

Before long, they exited the apiary and entered a long, whitewashed hallway that resembled an office complex. Room number after room number stretched on for what seemed like forever. The visual of endless department doors was broken only by the elevators that led to higher levels.

Their transporter pushed the button and said, "Once we get off the elevator, you will be in the grand Council room. I hope you realize what an honor this is."

Sparrow gulped as her throat tightened. "Yes, sir," she mumbled, her voice wavering in fear.

In a panic, she reached out and grabbed James'

hand, causing a shiver to run down his spine. He looked at her as she squeezed his palm, nearly crushing it. Her expression was glassy and distant, much like the face a soldier made when having a flashback.

He smiled as they stood hand in hand. There was a mix of pity and warmth rushing through his heart. He rubbed her finger with his thumb to get her attention. "Hey, don't worry. Everything will be all right."

"Thanks," she replied before looking down and noticing their hands locked together. Her cheeks grew red, and James was sure she was going to pull away, but much to his surprise, she held on until the elevator came to a halt. The next thing they knew, they were standing before the Council of the Heroes' Guild. The Council consisted of the five most powerful heroes as well as the five highest-ranking officials.

While James didn't recognize the officials, he definitely recognized the heroes. Dreadnaught was the hero sitting closest to him. With the power to manipulate light and energy in any fashion he desired, few enemies could escape his grasp. To his left was the Crimson Lady. She wore a blood-red jumpsuit and could drain the life force directly from a being's body. For that very reason, she was the most feared, and respected, woman in the entire world. To her left was Carl, the most nonchalant and ambivalent man in the world. With his power of never-ending good luck, he never had to lift a finger in order to bring his enemies to their knees. Next to him was Metamorphosis, a tall, slender woman who could transform into anyone or anything. Many a mob boss had had their plans foiled by her wily tricks.

Finally, there was Jeremy, James' brother. His hero name was Dauntless, and he boasted virtual invulnerability alongside immense strength. While he had other powers, it was for those two that he was feared and envied.

On the other side of the table sat the five highest-ranking officials in the Guild. All of them were older, grizzled, and worn-out-looking men and women. James felt very uncomfortable around them. Their sagging faces and bland, fitted suits made them look like clones and lent the room a corporate vibe.

Franklin waved for them to take their seats so the meeting could begin. "Now then, we are all here today at this meeting to discuss a matter of critical importance." He looked over at Sparrow. "I assume you informed him of the Nexus Orb?"

She nodded affirmatively. "Yes, Official Franklin, I filled him in on the basics."

Dreadnaught butted in before Franklin could respond. "All due respect, Franky, why are these two low-levels at this meeting? Shouldn't they be trying to track down a missing dog or something?"

James tensed up as his brother laughed alongside Dreadnaught. Kazav calmed James the best he could and after a deep breath, he regained control.

Franklin was in no mood for their antics and

raised his voice. "They are here because, despite their ranking, they have vital information to share. Information that they obtained despite great danger to themselves, so listen up!"

With the room now silent, Franklin motioned for Sparrow to stand and present her report. "Please, brief us on the situation."

"Thank you, Official Franklin," she replied as she walked to the podium. Once her binders were arranged to her liking, she dove into her presentation. "I am sorry to report that we have confirmed anti-hero activity taking place in our guild's patrol radius." She rifled through her binder and pulled out a photo that James had taken. It was an image of the odd symbol he observed while looking through their vans. Sparrow held it up for all to see. "All the districts who have reported this kind of activity confirm seeing the same symbol. It appears on the members' bags, clothes, and even their vehicles. Unfortunately, this suggests they are organized and widespread." She then pulled out an image of the factory James had tracked them into." Our investigation also confirms that they are using abandoned buildings for covert meetings."

"Where did you get these images?" asked one of the officials.

Sparrow looked to James, who gave her a modest grin. "One of our newer heroes bravely infiltrated a meeting and was able to gather some invaluable information."

"Right," Franklin barked out. "This budding

young hero, Night Phoenix, was able to track down and eavesdrop on these sinister zealots." He motioned for James to stand up and asked him to give a statement. The room gave him a halfhearted clap as he got up from his chair and thought of what to say.

"Night Phoenix?" Jeremy blurted out condescendingly. "That's a cute name, little bro."

Kazav could sense James getting riled up again. *"Stay cool, kid, just say a few words and then we can be done with this."*

He swallowed the lump building in his throat and gave a short remark. "Thank you all for your kind words. I was just serving the Guild and my community to the best of my abilities."

"So, little Sparrow," Jeremy called out. "Any other important details we should be made aware of?"

She scowled with an intensity James had never seen before. She didn't need to say a word in reply; everyone knew exactly what she was thinking. "Unfortunately, they seem to be aware of the Nexus Orb. They made mention of it during their meeting and appear to have a Corruption Crystal in their possession."

The mood in the room shifted markedly after hearing her mention the Orb and the Crystal.

"Seriously?" Jeremy cried aloud, his attention turning back to James. "Why didn't you take it away from them when you could have? Aren't you supposed to be a hero?"

Sparrow interrupted before he could scald

James any further. "He had no way of knowing what it was. The mission was strictly recon, and he performed his duties perfectly."

Dreadnaught slammed his fist on the table, leaving a massive dent on the steel surface. "So, what's our next move?"

Franklin stood up and motioned for Sparrow to take her seat. Once she was seated, he gave the room a rundown. "The next move is forming a dedicated task force to root out and eliminate this threat. Our first and most important objective is obtaining and destroying their Corruption Crystal. We also need to find out how they know about the Nexus Orb as it's possible the leak came from within the Guild itself."

Everyone began to look around the room at one another, a hint of suspicion now rising in the back of their minds.

"The next objective will be stepping up hero recruitment and training. If this new group of anti-hero zealots has a Corruption Crystal at their disposal, then monster activity is sure to spike."

The Crimson Lady leaned back in her chair and put her feet up on the desk. "That Corruption Crystal is what concerns me the most. I would like to volunteer myself to head up a task force dedicated to their destruction."

Franklin nodded in agreement. "You have experience with these Crystals, Crimson Lady, so that sounds like a solid plan."

After handing out tasks to the other heroes and officials, he turned his attention to James and Sparrow. "As for you two, I will be sending a detailed description of your new priorities once you return to your guildhall."

Sparrow saluted him and shouted, "Yes, sir! Thank you. We won't let you down."

A smile broke out on Franklin's face as Sparrow's enthusiasm filled him with vigor. "I know you won't! Now, everyone except the officials, please leave the Council room. We have much more to address before this day is over."

The high-level heroes left through a door at the other end of the room while James and Sparrow followed their assigned transporter back down to the arena floor.

"How do you think that went?" James asked Sparrow as they hurried along.

"The meeting? I think it went well. I'm excited about our new assignments, and I'm glad we had the chance to come here."

Now back in the room they had arrived in, the transporter held his hands out once again. They grabbed hold of him and got beamed back into the guildhall. Waiting to greet them was the entire team, eager to hear all about their time at HQ.

"Tell us everything!" Super Static squealed while tapping her feet on the floor excitedly.

Sparrow took a deep breath and sighed. "There

will be plenty of time to talk later today when we get our assignment from HQ. For now, I need to take a nap or something. I am exhausted." She swayed a bit as she shuffled out of the room to her quarters.

"Kid," Kazav mumbled amidst the drowning sounds of the team bickering and shouting. *"Let me know when you have a moment. There's something I want to show you."*

James made his way back to his room so that they could have some privacy. Once inside, Kazav instructed James to lay back in the bed and close his eyes.

"You're going to send me on another vision quest, aren't you?" James asked as he tensed up in anticipation.

"Just hold still and try not to ask too many questions."

The moment James' eyes shut; his mind was once again sent spiraling through the galaxy until it came to rest at Kazav's home planet. Things were far less painful compared to last time, something Kazav claimed was unavoidable, much to James' suspicion.

Kazav began to show James the events that took place after the first vision had ended. The two judges disappeared into the vast, swirling ocean of dark energy only for another figure to jump out. This once snuck across the obsidian rock and made their way over to Kazav, who was still restrained on the ground. The figure embraced Kazav and began to free him of his bindings. Once he was no longer shackled, they spoke to one another in soothing, subtle vibrations.

"Could you translate this like before?" James asked Kazav, hoping to hear what was being said.

"I'd rather not," he replied. The words he spoke were tender and affectionate, and Kazav preferred to keep his personal life private.

Standing up, the figures embraced once more before Kazav flew off the surface of the planet and out into space. After some time passed, a new planet came into view, a familiar one.

James realized that what he was seeing was Kazav discovering his planet. *"Oh, so this all happened just before we met?"*

"Yes, this is how I got free of my confinement and made my way to your world."

The vision ended, and James sat back up in bed. "Who was that person who helped you? You seemed very close."

"She is my, uh, girlfriend, I suppose you could call it. There isn't a term on your planet that can be applied to the relationship me and her share. That is the closest wording I can think of."

James smirked. Kazav having feelings? That was too good a discovery to leave unteased. "So, is it love?"

Kazav became defensive. *"Is what love?"*

"What you and that girlfriend of yours share. Is it love?"

Kazav let out a deep sigh. *"No questions right*

now, kid, I'm not in the mood."

Just before he could really grill Kazav, Sparrow knocked on the door. "Guild meeting in five minutes!" she shouted from the other side.

"Be right out!" James yelled back. "Don't think this is over, Kazav. I still have a ton of questions about you and your mystery girl."

Kazav groaned. *"I knew I shouldn't have shown you. That's what I get for opening up."*

Once James was back in his seat, Sparrow began the briefing. "Listen up, team! The Heroes' Guild has determined that a new threat is growing within our city, an unknown organization with sinister object-ives." Pointing to the screen behind her, she began to list out the directives sent from HQ. "The first object-ive is to gather as much information as possible. The more we know about the enemy, the better equipped we are to fight them."

She clicked on her keypad and brought up the next screen. A graph showing their retainment num-bers popped up with a somber filter. "We also need to step up recruitment and bolster our numbers. We need more heroes patrolling the neighborhood while we handle the bigger threats."

The next few slides were images of items and paraphernalia James had photographed during his mission. "Finally, we need a dedicated task force to root out and eliminate both the cultist's leaders as well as their Corruption Crystals."

"Woah, hold the phone!" Owl blurted out. "Corruption Crystals? That's crazy!"

Super Static tugged on Sparrow's arm. "This is bigger than you're letting on, isn't it?"

With both hands on the desk, Sparrow leaned over and sighed. "I won't lie to you all, things are bad. HQ is very concerned about this new threat, and what's worse is we know so little about it."

Falcon chimed in with a question. "Aren't they the same weirdos who tried turning everyone into fish?"

Hawk shook his head. "Nah, you're thinking of the Fishermen cult. Those guys wore trout masks on their heads."

"Nuh-uh!" Falcon cried out. "You're thinking of the Trout Clout Gang. These guys are totally different."

Hawk's eyes narrowed in frustration. "Why are you always tryna show me up, bro?"

Falcon's eyes followed suit. "I'm not showing you up, dude. I'm just saying you gotta stop mixing up your gangs and your fish!"

Sparrow rolled her eyes. This was not the first meeting to be derailed by their stupidity.

Hawk stood up and started poking Falcon with his finger. "So, I'm supposed to be an expert on North Atlantic fish species now, is that it?"

Falcon stood up and poked him back. "I'm just saying trout and salmon are very recognizable. You see a salmon-"

Sparrow slammed her hands on the desk before he could finish. "Enough!" she shouted. "Put your fish debate on the back burner, boys, this is far more important, and we have limited time to act!"

Sitting back down, they pouted and nodded. "Sorry, ma'am."

James couldn't help but smile at their exchanges. They reminded him of when he and Jeremy were younger, back when they still got along.

"Now then," Sparrow continued, "I want Owl and Super Static to head a task force regarding the elimination of the Corruption Crystals. Falcon and I will start hunting down high-profile targets in our precinct while Hawk and Night Phoenix do the same."

James looked over at Hawk, who gave him a nod and a finger gun.

Sparrow shut her computer off and stood up. "If anyone has any questions, come to me, and I'll try to help in any way I can. Otherwise, this meeting is over."

Owl and Super Static had some concerns for Sparrow, so they followed her out of the room. Hawk stood up and slapped James on the back. "You ready to work with the best?" he asked in all seriousness.

James let out a chuckle as Hawk postured. "Definitely, it should be fun!"

"Sparrow sent me the name of our first target." He pulled out his phone and brought up an image of the monster. "Looks like they're calling it Steel Skin because bullets just bounce right of 'em."

James snuck a peek. He thought it looked like a deformed humanoid that fell into a blender.

"It was last located in sector C," Hawk informed him. "I recommend we head out now while the sun is still up."

They geared up and met outside, where Hawk gave James a piece of advice. "I know there is a lot to worry about right now, James, but try to block all that out of your head. When fighting a monster as dangerous as Steel Skin, you don't have any opportunities to be distracted. One false step, and it's game over, you understand?"

James nodded. "Got it. I won't let you down."

Hawk gave him another smack and said, "I know you won't. Now let's go get 'em!"

Having traversed half the city, they came to rest atop the tallest building in sector C. From this vantage point, they could look around for miles in all directions.

As they took in the city from on high, James asked, "Now what?"

With his gaze unbroken, Hawk replied, "Now we keep an eye out and see if anything catches our attention."

While they waited, James watched Hawk with unspoken awe. His appearance was that of a bird of prey, and his mannerisms matched the look. His golden eyes were slitted like a bird, and most of his costume was outfitted with avian-based decorations. A necklace hung down to his chest with a razor-sharp beak at the end. Feathers jutted out from parts of his suit and gave it a sleek and predatorial aura.

"So," James said, breaking the silence. "Are you and Falcon brothers?"

Haw chuckled at the question. "Not by blood, but in a manner of speaking, yes, we are brothers. We grew up together, went to the same foster home, and when we lost our foster parents, we both ended up on the streets. That's when we made a pact to look out for each other, no matter what."

That was not the backstory James was expecting. He always felt Hawk and Falcon behaved like spoiled frat boys, not parentless orphans. "So how did you work your way into the Guild?"

"Falcon and I used our powers to rob people, but eventually we got involved with some mob types and got into major trouble with the law. The Guild heard about it and offered us a deal: use our power for good, or rot in jail. How about you?" Hawk asked, hoping to draw attention off himself. "You got any siblings?"

The question hit him hard. James didn't like to talk about Jeremy, especially after their last exchange. "Just one. An older brother. Our relationship is...complicated."

"I get it. Family can be a tricky situation. Sometimes I want to smack Falcon upside the head and other times I can't imagine my life without him. That's family, I suppose."

James let out a laugh. "You can say that again."

Now feeling melancholy, they went back to observing the city in silence.

Little time had passed before Hawk's attention turned to the streets. Tilting his head, he strained to locate the source.

James watched as Hawk angled his head from one side to the other. "What is it?"

"Listen," Hawk instructed. "Don't you hear that?"

With great effort, James was able to pick up the sounds of crashing, smashing, and screaming, rising from the streets below. "I hear it. Let's go!"

Both jumped out over the edge and while James fell like a brick, Hawk soared out overhead, his arms now turned into powerful wings. With the power to morph into a hawk at will, he could soar through the sky unimpeded by gravity.

James admired Hawk's awesome form as he plummeted to the ground, hoping that someday he could fly as masterfully as Hawk. Before he met the ground, a massive pair of talons gripped him and carried him along in flight. James looked up to see Hawk in full bird form, flapping his massive wings as he let out a deafening screech.

"You see him?" Hawk asked through the deafening roar of the air.

James scanned the ground below until he located the source of the commotion. "Yup, I see it."

"All right, I'm gonna send you right at him," Hawk told him as he shot up further into the sky. The force of the climb was causing James' stomach to sink, like when an airplane took off.

Now far above the ground, Hawk stopped rising. Bringing his wings against his body, they entered a free fall. With a sonic boom, they dove downward, forcing James' face to flap and contort with the wind.

Then, with incredible precision, Hawk released James from his grip, sending him flying like a bullet directly into the monster. The initial impact sent out a shockwave, shattering all the glass on the nearby cars and buildings.

Once through the street level, they kept smashing past layer after layer of the city's infrastructure. First the street, then the sewers, then the sub-level, until they broke through the bedrock, sending cracks into the solid earth.

The moment they stopped descending, the monster sent a kick into James' stomach, forcing the air out of his lungs and sending a rippling shock through his body. The force of the blow sent him flying back up through the hole they had created and nearly into Hawk, who was circling above. Swooping in, he caught James before he went up too far and dropped him off back on the ground.

"You okay, brother?" he asked James as he morphed back into a human.

He coughed and caught his breath. "Yeah, I'll be

okay. Thanks."

With a howl, Steel Skin jumped up to the surface and began to sprint at them, claws outstretched.

Hawk didn't wait for it to close the gap. He darted forward, sending blow after blow against the monster's infamous steel pelt, with little effect. The beast let out a garbled laugh as Hawk's strikes failed to do it any harm.

With one swift flick of its arm, it sent Hawk flying through an apartment building. James rushed in with a flurry of fast kicks. So fast were his strikes, it sounded as though a machine gun was being unloaded. Steel Skin absorbed everything and attempted to send him flying as it did to Hawk. Dodging its claws, James leapt back, creating some distance between them.

Hawk flew back onto the scene in bird form and let out a massive gust of wind from his wings, sending Steel Skin tumbling backward. James took the opportunity to pick up a busted fire hydrant off the ground and use it as a giant club. Swing after swing, he smacked it into the monster, sending it crashing through streetlights, stop signs, and whoever's car was unlucky enough to be in the way. While the force of the blows was enough to irk the beast, it was still not causing any real damage, and before long, the club was reduced to a jagged, bent metal pole.

Hawk could see they needed a new tactic, so, grabbing the monster in his talons, he lifted it skyward. The beast wriggled but was unable to break free of Hawk's razor-sharp claws. He got Steel Skin up thousands of feet, then let it drop.

A moment later, he began an aerial dive and closed in on his target. He dashed and slashed into the monster repeatedly, sending it jerking back and forth through the sky. It was unclear if it was having any effect until the monster came crashing to the ground covered in gouges. Hawk was able to pierce its armored skin, but most of the cuts were superficial and served only to enrage the beast.

Now on the offensive, it sent a flurry of clawed strikes against James, who was able to deflect and absorb most of the blows. Countering one of the creature's swings, he smacked it back into the air where Hawk was waiting, ready to send another wave of talon attacks into the monster's robust skin.

Once Hawk was finished, he sent the creature rocketing down to the ground along with a volley of razor-sharp feathers he let loose from his wings. The feathers turned into deadly darts, pelting the pavement as well as the beast.

Now in a full-on, adrenaline-fueled rampage, the monster came running out on all fours, taking James completely by surprise. A full-force punch to his head sent James flying, forcing him to bounce off a streetlight and into a bus. The monster jumped on top of him and clawed at him manically. James guarded his head with his arms and hands, letting his torso take most of the damage.

"Kazav!" James cried out. "Can't we do something?"

"Hang on, kid," he shouted back. *"I think we might be well enough along in our bond to show this freak something new!"*

Suddenly, James felt flush with power. The air around him glowed a dark, dangerous aura. Stopping the monster's assault mid-blow, his hand cooked the creature's skin, sending black burns climbing up its arms. With a swift crack of his fist, he forced it back, a sizzling black mark growing across its skin.

James looked down at his hands. They shimmered as dark, plasma-like energy flowed across his fingers. *"What's happening, Kazav?"*

"The next level, kid, that's what's happening!"

"The next level?" James repeated as the monster writhed on the ground in pain. *"I like the sound of that!"*

With immense force, James jumped forward, extending his leg out for a devastating kick. The monster managed to avoid him, but not before being burnt once again by the heat radiating off his foot.

"This is awesome!" James cried out, as the ground beneath his foot turned into a scorched pile of cinders.

Kazav cackled with excitement. *"Agreed, kid, agreed!"*

The monster was regaining its composure and shot back toward James. With his new ability in tow, he took a solid stance and charged up his fist. Hawk attempted to swoop in and halt the monster's advance, but he was too far away.

James pulled back his fist and, once the monster was in range, let out a strike that sent molten flames shooting through its body. Awash in a sea of burning plasma, the monster flew backward and came to rest in the remains of a building that had been vaporized from the heat.

Hawk turned back into human form and stood behind James. "Wow," he remarked. "I've never seen anything like that before."

James stood there motionless, still in shock from the power of his attack. "Yeah," he mumbled. "Me neither."

They made sure the monster was dispatched, then brought it back to the guildhall so Bella could perform some tests. James returned to his room and played around with his new ability. After showing it off to Sparrow and the rest of the team, he decided he would incorporate it into his daily training sessions.

"You keep this up," Sparrow teased, "and you are well on your way to the top twenty."

James smiled. The top twenty would be a dream come true. "You really think?

She gave him a wink and added, "With a team like this, anything is possible."

11/SUPER STATIC

Hawk and James kept the peace in the city the best they could. Several weeks passed as they worked side by side, growing in power and trust. The previous day, Sparrow had announced there would be a change to the team's groupings and instructed everyone to meet in the main hall for a task reassignment.

James sat somewhat slumped in his chair, a pounding headache coursing through his skull from last night's fight, as Sparrow gave an update on the situation. "Nice work, Owl and Super Static, on taking out one of the cultist chapters and recovering a Corruption Crystal."

The table cheered at the news; James winced as the noise added to his misery.

"Hawk and Night Phoenix, you have been doing a great job on keeping crime and monster attack numbers down." Hawk threw up a peace sign and grinned in satisfaction. "However," Sparrow continued, "collateral damage has been high, and the mayor is breathing down my neck to lower the cost your fights have on the city."

"How are we supposed to control that?" Hawk cried out.

Sparrow snapped her gaze to him and let out a sigh. "I know it's not completely under your control, but it may be a good idea to switch the teams up a bit. So, Owl and Falcon, you are on patrol duty. Hawk can come with me. Night Phoenix and Super Static, I want you two to continue with the anti-hero group investigation."

"Yes, ma'am," Super Static chirped.

James gave Sparrow a thumbs-up and rolled his chair over to Static. She began to lay out the game plan that she and Owl had established as well as update him on the progress they made. "We managed to capture a member of this strange new organization. He has refused to give us any information. However, we were able to extract some information from his belongings."

James looked over the documents they had recovered while Super Static munched on a graham cracker. Crumbs fell all over the desk as she devoured the entire pack.

"This report states they're using Corruption Crystals to create and strengthen monsters." He raised an eyebrow. "How exactly does that happen?"

Static threw the empty box of crackers behind her. They missed the trashcan by a mile and landed on the floor. "The Crystals seem to activate a corruption process within the DNA of living beings. Depending on their resistance to the Crystals' influence, they will either turn into a monster or resist its power."

James grew a little concerned. When he looked at the Corruption Crystal, he felt the strangest urge to touch it. He began to wonder what that meant for him.

Static noticed he was becoming agitated and motioned for him to take a cracker. James declined but was appreciative of the offer. Static had a reputation of only offering food to people she liked, so James took that as a good sign.

"What is the best way to go about tracking these Crystals down?" James asked, hoping to take his mind off his insecurities.

Static tore into another box of crackers and began speaking with her mouth half full. "Honestly, we just try talking to people, asking contacts and informants if they know anything. We got lucky a few days ago and the tip we got turned into discovering an actual meeting location."

She rifled through a bag and started laying out items found at the scene. It was everything you would expect from a cult-like organization. Robes, candles, sacred texts. Static pulled the last item out of the bag: a Corruption Crystal fragment.

James' eyes dilated as he gazed upon the sleek, quartz-like crystal rolling around in her hand. "You okay, James?" Static asked, forcing him to snap back to his senses. "You look a bit glassy-eyed."

"Huh? Yeah, I'm fine! I think I just overdid it yesterday. The fight me and Hawk got into was pretty intense."

"Oh, that's right!" she recalled. "You have those new, epic fire powers, right?"

James chuckled. "Yeah, it's pretty sweet! I like calling it black plasma because, well, it sounds cooler if you ask me."

She shook her head up and down. "I totally agree."

Then, leaping from her chair, she wiped the crumbs off her suit and grabbed James by the arm. "Let's head out! We got a lead that the group has been trying to recruit inmates from local prisons. We gotta look into that."

They headed to the prison on the outskirts of town. It was an isolated, run-down detainment center that was notorious for its poor conditions and bad treatment of the prisoners. After running through the forest that surrounded the facility, Static waved at the front gate for them to let her in. A few minutes passed, but the gate remained shut.

"Huh," she huffed as they stood there in the open. "They knew to expect me. I wonder why they won't open the gate."

James looked up at the guard posts, then out into the yard. It was unnaturally quiet, and not a single person was in sight. Static motioned for James to follow her around the back. Once they arrived, they were greeted by a massive hole in the back wall.

"What in the world?" Static mouthed.

James poked her shoulder and pointed out into

the forest. A trail of monster footprints led out into the woods and had forced down trees and vegetation.

Static looked back and forth at the prison and the pathway. "Let's check out the prison first, then we can follow up on the tracks."

He nodded and ran after her as she vaulted over the broken section of the wall.

Once inside, they started their investigation. James felt like he needed a tetanus shot just by being so close to all the jagged, rusty metal bars, many of which had been torn off their hinges and tossed onto the ground. "Whoever did this was very strong," James remarked as he stepped over one of the broken cell doors.

"For sure," Static whispered. "Let's keep a sharp eye."

While James waded through the crusty, dilapidated cell blocks, light from cracks in the ceiling filtered in, illuminating the facility in a haunting, yet beautiful glow.

"What happened to all the inmates?" James asked while keeping close to Static.

"No idea," she replied. "Let's just keep our wits about us. I get the feeling those monsters won't be gone for long."

Using her power, she created a ball of electricity in her hand, lighting up the dark hallway they were currently venturing through.

James could detect an odd cluster of feelings

seeping out from Kazav. It was a mix of sadness, anger, and disgust. *"You okay, buddy?"*

"Yeah, I'm fine," he mumbled sullenly. *"This place just reminds me of being locked up back in my home world. Just be glad you only live for about eighty years or so. Being locked up for thousands is a fate worse than death."*

After they had made it through the cell blocks, they entered the cafeteria, which was covered in a layer of dust. Stacks of clothing were piled up in the corners of the room alongside chains, cuffs, and other prison equipment. Footprints in the thick, snow-like powder revealed monster tracks interspersed with human.

"What happened in here?" James asked, his voice cracking in the dry, dusty air.

"Monster conversion," Static informed as she pointed to the tracks. "They used the Corruption Crystal to turn all the prisoners into monsters."

"What's with all the dust?"

Taking a handful of the powder from the ground, Static revealed a disgusting truth. "When an individual's body rejects the transformation process, they turn into dust."

"So, what you're saying is all this stuff floating through the air is dead people?"

She nodded. James gagged a bit before covering his face with a cloth.

Their investigation was cut short by the sound

of trees snapping in the distance. Something was coming their way, something big. The walls of the cafeteria were torn down as a thirty-foot-tall monster burst through, letting out an animalistic howl. With the head of a deer and the body of a morbidly deformed human, this creature shot to the top five of the most horrendous-looking beasts James had ever seen.

As its rancid breath filled the room, Static plugged her nose and took a battle stance. The beast waved its head back and forth with its antlers on full display, a clear sign of aggression.

Super Static began to glow, arcs of electricity bouncing across her body. "All right, you overgrown reindeer!" she shouted. "Come get some!"

With her hands outstretched, she let out a barrage of lightning strikes that sent thunderous booms echoing across the valley. The monster bellowed and howled but kept moving forward despite the intensity of her assault. James joined in the fray by dashing past the monster and chucking fallen trees at the beast's back, forcing it to turn its attention outside.

"Keep it busy," Static called out to James. "I need to charge and can't afford an interruption."

"Got it!" he shouted back while sending a mossy rock flying at the beast's face.

It closed in, attempting to smash him with its oversized fists, but the monster was slow, and he could easily avoid its strikes. A few minutes passed with James evading the monster as it eagerly tried to pound him into the dirt.

"I'm ready!" Static shouted. "Bring it closer! I can't afford to miss!"

Like a plasma ball, arcs of electricity flowed around her in a majestic torrent, encasing her in glowing blue light. Now within striking distance, Static let loose every volt she had, bathing the creature in a torrent of lightning.

Falling to its knees, it cried out as its fur caught fire and its flesh cooked from the heat. With a strained grunt, she let out a final wave of power before the lightning stopped and the air grew silent.

Wavering, she leaned to one side and began to fall over, her power now fully drained. James ran over to her and supported her head off the ground. "Are you okay?" he asked as she stared back up at him, glassy-eyed. Her eyes went wide as she looked past him, prompting him to turn around.

He flipped just in time to see the beast bring its massive arms crashing down on them. Instinctively, James brought his hands up and halted the monster's fists before they could accomplish their grizzly goal.

He shouted for Static to get to a safe distance so he could deal with the creature and allow her the space to recover. Once she was out of harm's way, he flung the monster's arms back up and slammed into its knee with a swift and powerful kick.

More enraged than ever, the beast started another series of punches aimed at James, who dodged and weaved between them while charging up an attack of his own. Once it was overextended, James launched up to its face and let out a fierce plasma blow, teeth flying out into the tall grass.

With the beast reeling, James leapt into the air and began to spin rapidly. Now falling, he extended his foot and sent it crashing into the monster's shoulder. Loud cracks and pops confirmed the extent of the damage and the creature fell over, its spine no longer in one piece.

With the immediate danger now passed, Static shuffled over to examine the beast. "Wow, you turned this thing's back into loose gravel!"

"Thanks. I suppose all that training has been paying off."

Static charged up her hand and sent one last lightning bolt directly into the monster's head. Satisfied that it was dead, she leaned over to James and said, "Just checking."

She cracked off one of the antlers for Bella to examine and motioned for James to follow her.

"Where are we going?"

"Back to the guildhall. Sparrow is gonna want to know about what went down here. If they are planning on hitting the other prisons, then we have a real problem brewing."

Exhausted from her devastating attack, Sparrow leaned against James, limiting the speed at which they could travel. "You seem to be enjoying hero life," she said, noting his progress.

"Yeah." He chuckled. "Although, it is a bit more painful than I was hoping."

She let out a giggle and squeezed his arm. "True, but you look like you can take a beating."

"Speaking of compliments, what you did back there was amazing! I half-expected the monster to be vaporized from the raw power of your lightning strike."

"Thank you! Who would have thought electricity is useful for more than just giving people carpet shocks?" she joked as her voice trailed off.

They walked in silence for a while. Static was still weak from the battle, and James was not exactly gifted with small talk. "So, why did you want to join the Guild?" he asked, hoping it was enough to jump-start the conversation.

She stopped walking and faced him. In a serious tone, she stated, "If you ever ask me that again, I'm afraid I'll have to kill you."

James stammered, afraid he had somehow crossed a line. "No, no... I didn't mean... I'm sorry if-"

He stopped floundering as a smile grew on her face, revealing she had been teasing him.

"That wasn't very nice," he remarked, the concern vanishing.

She giggled. "You're gonna have to get used to the teasing. It's how I communicate with my friends."

James let out an awkward laugh while Static snorted in amusement. "Gotcha. I'll keep that in mind."

Once the joy of teasing him faded, her face grew sullen and melancholy. "Well, I don't have a sob story like Hawk or Sparrow if that's what you're wondering. My life was normal compared to most other heroes. I had good parents, no siblings, went to school, and got good grades. Once my powers manifested, I had two options: live a mundane and boring life, or live a life full of action and adventure. I chose the latter."

James smiled and nodded as she spoke. He knew there was a lot she was keeping to herself, something dark and painful, but he was not looking to pry.

"So how about you?" she asked. "Have you always wanted to be a hero?"

James took a moment to think about how to word things. He was not, after all, a real hero and didn't manifest his powers naturally. "Hmm, well, I guess my story is like yours. I had a decent family life, went to school, got a job. I guess the difference between us is I did live a boring life before I joined."

"What made you change your mind?"

A pensive feeling built inside him. He thought back to all the times in his life he wished he could have been a real hero, all the moments he wished he could change things for the better. "I suppose I just got tired of being ordinary."

She nodded, impressed with its simple eloquence. "That is a really good answer," she admitted. Letting go of his arm, she stood on her own and let out a massive yawn. "Wow, I'm starving! What say we pick up the pace and get back to the Guild so I can destroy the pantry?"

James grinned as she took off running. "Yeah, after eating all those crackers, you must be famished."

She placed her hand on her stomach and gave it a rub. "I'm a big girl. I gotta eat."

They made it back to the Guild before sundown and as promised, Static went on a carb bender. Only when she passed out in a food coma did her rampage end.

12/OWL

Sparrow kept them together for a few weeks, spying on the other prisons in case they got hit. It was mostly uneventful aside from the occasional monster attack. Due to the lack of activity, Sparrow teamed up with Static and had James pair up with Owl for a special assignment.

Alone in the guildhall, James waited for him to drop down from the rafters. He often wondered why he wasn't called Bat. Hanging upside down, staying up all night, that was all bat stuff, right?

Like clockwork, morning arrived, and Owl flipped down from the rafters, landing without a sound. Staring deep into James' eyes, he issued a foreboding warning. "Prepare yourself for the battle, young hero. This one may well be your last." He then took off running out the door, providing no commands or context.

James sat in silence, unsure of what to do. *"Uh... okay? Was I supposed to follow him? Or should I just wait here?"*

"Hmm," Kazav grumbled. *"I no longer sense him in the building, so safe money on follow."*

James scurried out the door and caught up to

Owl.

"What an odd follow," he mused as he watched Owl leap across the city skyline with silent grace and dignity. James likened it to water flowing between the rocks and ridges of a stream. While everyone else pivoted and jerked about when they ran the roofs, Owl was meticulous, like every step was carefully considered. "Where are we heading?" James shouted as the wind drowned out his voice.

"To our grave, if we are not careful," Owl replied portentously. Then, while stopped atop the roof of an abandoned factory, he took in a deep breath. "Ah," he sighed. "This will do nicely."

"What will do nicely?"

Owl pointed to a garbage dump off in the distance. "The beast relies on smell. If you muddle its senses, the advantage is ours."

"Oh, you want us to go in there?" he asked, apprehensive of the response. Owl confirmed his fears with a nod. "Great, can't wait to go dumpster diving."

Now walking among piles of trash, James held his breath while taking in the skeptic scene. Rainbow-streaked streams pooled in the dirt, flowing throughout the dumping grounds like caustic rivers. Rats scurried up and down the walkways as they carried moldy foods back to their dens. Owl had no problem getting dirty and leapt atop a heap of trash, picking out baubles and trinkets, keeping them if he liked them or tossing them back if he didn't.

James looked on in disgust. "Are you looking for something, buddy?"

"Anything and everything," Owl chirped excitedly while flinging broken ceramic plates off the pile and onto the ground below.

The smell was overpowering, and James could barely keep from gagging. *"Kazav, I'm begging you, please turn off my nose!"*

He mercifully reduced James' olfactory abilities. *"I'm with you on this one, kid. This place smells downright awful."*

"Thanks, for being less of a sadistic jerk than usual."

The feeling of being watched grew as the day stretched on. *"Keep your wits about you, kid,"* Kazav warned. "Something big is coming your way, something angry."

James gulped as his throat tightened in anticipation. Between Owl's ominous warning and Kazav's genuine concern, he was starting to get worried. "Hey, Owl," he called out into the junkyard. "This monster we're hunting, what's the story behind it?"

He jumped out from behind a stack of magazines with a tattered issue of *Avian Monthly* in his hands. "This beast, it's a scientific and medical abomination."

Images of Frankenstein-like creatures flashed through James' head. "What do you mean?"

Owl sat on a rubber tire and explained while

flipping through the magazine. "This creature is made by warping an already hyper-corrupt being with a Corruption Crystal to the point of insanity. So basically, it's a monster even to other monsters."

His tone was confusing, and James was starting to grow impatient. "So, how concerned should we be?"

"Oh, very!" he barked while turning a page. Then, in true Owl form, he casually added, "We may both die here today."

Kazav was getting irritated. *"This guy is an airhead! Is he like this on purpose?"*

James laughed as he watched Owl sprawl out on the ground and rifle through another issue. *"I know he is a bit strange, but it's usually the odd ones that hide the most amazing talents. I'm sure Owl is more capable than he seems, even if he is an oddball with a bird obsession."*

"Oddball with a bird obsession?" Kazav repeated. *"You said that series of words way too casually."*

Once the last ray of sunlight vanished behind the horizon, a tingle ran down James' spine. In the distance, he could detect the faint sounds of people screaming alongside a ferocious grunting as the monster made its way through the city and over to the junkyard. As it got closer, Owl too could detect the beast's proximity and dove out of sight.

Staying silent, they went hyper-alert, twitching and jumping at every little noise. James nearly jumped out of his skin when a loud crash erupted from behind. Turning his head, he looked over to see the monster sitting atop a mound of refuse, hunkered over while taking in long, deep breaths. It knew they were here; it just couldn't see them yet.

Crouched behind an abandoned car, James took in the monster's wicked form. It resembled a cougar, only it had scales and rows of needle-like teeth. Massive, jagged claws protruded out of each of its three toes, and a row of spiny ridges extended from head to tail.

James felt trapped, unsure of what to do. If he moved, the beast might see him, but if he stayed still, it would probably sniff him out anyway. Owl had already started to position himself for an attack. He hovered above the monster in midair, silent as an Owl in flight, and motioned for James to make his way behind the beast.

James threw a can to cause a distraction, giving him enough time to move from his current position to the one Owl was suggesting. With a series of silent hand gestures that they rehearsed in training; Owl signed for James to restrain the monster so he could unleash a powerful blow. James gave him a thumbs up, shuddering as he did. The plan would mean he would have to not only get close to the monster but hold it in place.

James decided to rip off the Band-Aid and latch on to the beast as tight as possible. With lightning speed, he reached out and grabbed the monster from behind, wrapping himself around its arms and waist while giving it the tightest bear hug of its life. It let out a demented, ear-piercing howl as it jumped around trying to buck James off its back. He held on as best he could and tried to keep it below Owl, who was still charging his strike.

The air began to vibrate like water next to a speaker. Sound waves pulsed out from Owl's chest, increasing in frequency as the power built inside his lungs. Now ready, he shouted, "Hold it still!" James clung to the monster, trying not to get flung off its bony back.

Smashing the creature's feet into the ground to prevent movement, James dove out of the way, giving Owl the all-clear to unleash his full power.

Owl swooped in and grabbed hold of the beast while a swell of power worked up from his lungs, pooling in his throat. Finally, he opened his mouth, letting out an eruption of air-distorting soundwaves directly into the monster's head. Even with his ears covered, James could hardly keep from screaming as the mind-melting vibrations flew out in all directions. At point-blank range, the monster was taking the brunt of it, letting out warped howls as the pain raced through its mind. After what felt like forever, Owl finished his attack, letting out a parting kick that sent the beast flying through countless piles of trash.

James uncovered his ears and shook his head. Once his vision stopped splitting, he looked on in awe at the destructive power of Owl's abilities. As far as the eye could see, a massive hole had been torn through the landscape. The force of his soundwave attack was so intense, and so focused, that whatever stood in its way was turned to rubble.

Despite the ferocity of the blow, the monster recovered, sprinting at them with claws outstretched, eager to exact revenge. A back and forth of attacks and counterattacks ensued, slowly turning into an ordeal as the beast became skilled at deflecting their moves. Now on the offensive, the monster unleashed a series of clawed strikes, swiping at James with both its arms and inflicting deep, painful wounds.

Owl was able to send it flying back with a palm strike, but the blow hardly made it flinch. "This is unsustainable!" he shouted as he huffed from fatigue.

Kazav chimed in with a suggestion. *"Kid, this beast, it's gotta have a weak spot. Try to single out a target area and strike with more precision."*

James tried examining the creature further while Owl kept it at bay, pelting its hide with precise blasts of his sonic voice. After failing to find a weak spot, James had an inspiration. If it didn't have a weak spot outside its body, then maybe he should attack it from the inside.

He manipulated the dark, burning energy that coursed through his veins, focusing it in his fist. *"Do you think this will work?"* he asked Kazav as his fist grew red and began to glow.

"No idea! Let's find out!"

With every bit of speed he could muster, James flanked the monster from behind. Then, with a crimson glow, he slammed his fist into the beast's armored back, sending chunks of its plating flying off in every direction. Like lightning scars on a victim's skin, red veins crept throughout its hide, searing its supple flesh from the inside. Attempting to finish the beast while it was down, Owl ran forward and leaped into the air only to be blasted by a beam of energy from the creature's mouth.

James tried to reach Owl, who was now lying motionless on the ground, but the monster afforded him no opportunity as it shot off blast after blast of deadly energy from its gullet. Even just in passing, they caused James' skin to burn and blister.

After a beam nearly struck his face, he instinctively deflected it, allowing him to realize he could also manipulate energy attacks sent at him by his opponents.

With newfound confidence, he stood at the ready for the monster to fire another shot, eager to test his theory. Sure enough, it fired another beam and with his arms outstretched, he caught it before it could make contact. Then, sending it back, he blasted it into the monster's shoulder, forcing it to lose its balance.

Before he could close the gap, the monster let out a sustained blast of energy to vaporize James completely. With his hands held up like a shield, the energy stream split in two, bypassing him and leaving the ground behind scorched in its wake.

Now completely exhausted, the monster cut off

the beam and let out a fatigued growl. Having spent most of its power, it tried to crawl away as James steadily approached. With his hands charged and ready, he raised them, aimed at the monster's face, and let loose all that he had.

The junkyard was lit up for miles around as a blue and black stream of molten plasma flowed from his hands. The monster disappeared into the torrent of burning power, letting out screams of agony as it was cooked inside its chitinous shell.

With nothing left of the beast but a scorched skeleton, James rushed over to check on Owl. "Hey! Are you okay?" he asked frantically.

Owl rolled over and groaned. Once he saw the monster had been dispatched, he whipped a magazine out and began to flip through the pages.

James let out a relieved sigh. "I'll take that as a yes."

13/PANIC

Months of grueling combat flew by, and with each new battle, James' powers became more refined, lending him a deadly edge.

With his skills becoming known citywide, Sparrow feared that he intended to leave his posting at her guild and request a transfer to the inner city where the opportunities for advancement were more lucrative. He was a topic she found herself dwelling on more each day, much to her concern. She tried to figure out what it was about him that she felt so...drawn to. Was he handsome? Sure, but that was never her focus. What she really liked was his heart, his inner self. The more missions they went on together, the more she got to see all the different sides of his personality.

James found himself getting drawn to Sparrow as well. She was, of course, very beautiful. But for him, that was a delightful bonus. She had a sincerity about her that made him feel comfortable, like he could tell her anything. Kazav noticed all this and tried to keep James focused on hero business. This was the kind of danger he was hoping to avoid, a distraction that would keep James from realizing his full potential.

One day, after training, the team met in the

main hall for an urgent update. This message was rumored to have come straight from HQ and had everyone buzzing.

"Everyone, please calm down!" Sparrow shouted. Her plea fell on deaf ears as Falcon and Hawk let the room devolve into a pointless debate.

"Water is wet!" Falcon stated confidently.

"Not true, not true!" Hawk disagreed.

"It is so!" Falcon then regaled the room with an explanation. "It's wet because it makes you feel wet! Therefore, it is, by its very nature, wet!"

Hawk slammed his hand on the table. "That's just faulty logic!" he cried out. "Does that mean that lava is wet if it makes you feel wet?"

Falcon let out a condescending laugh. "Are you kidding me right now? The two things are completely different! Besides, lava feels hot, not wet."

Super Static chimed in with her own opinion. "If it's all about how it makes you feel, then water isn't wet because feeling is relative to the individual."

Hawk leaned over the table and high-fived her. "Tell it how it is, Static!"

Owl fell from the ceiling where he was napping and gave his two cents. "Well, seeing as how you all woke me with your inane chatter, I figure I should add some culture to this conversation."

Everyone waited for him to speak as he stood there motionless. Then, in a very anticlimactic manner, announced, "Water is wet."

The room erupted into chaos. Everyone talked among themselves as Sparrow sat in her chair, defeated.

Their attention broke when James opened the doors to the hall. He walked in apprehensively, first looking at his teammates, then at Sparrow, who had her face buried in her hands. After an awkward shuffle to his chair, he stated, "There is a really weird energy in this room right now."

Taking advantage of the lapse in conversation, Sparrow shot up and began the briefing. "Thank you all for assembling so...promptly. We have a lot to talk about. We also have a high-priority message from HQ that all the guildhalls should be getting any moment now. They are live-streaming it to everyone, so it must be big."

Super Static raised her hand, waiting to talk until called on. "What's the message about?"

Sparrow shrugged. "I have no idea. Nobody has told me anything."

Everyone started to murmur about what kind of update to expect. Some thought it was good news, others bad.

"I heard they're telling us that we got 'em all," Falcon said, forcing all attention on himself.

Hawk let out a sarcastic laugh. "There's no way that's true."

Falcon's smile morphed into a scowl. "Why do you always have to disagree with me, Hawk?"

"Why are you always wrong?"

Sparrow slammed her hand down on the desk. "Enough!" she shouted. Composing herself, she lowered her voice and added, "There are a lot of rumors right now, but none of them have any merit. Let's just wait for HQ and hope for the best. Okay?

Everyone nodded as the room fell into silence. Sparrow looked over at James, who silently mouthed, "Wow," causing her to smirk and shake her head.

The group was acting more like a family every day, which, unfortunately, included bickering. The silence of the room was shattered by a notification. Everyone looked at the blue screen, which was now setting up a secure connection. Sparrow prodded everyone to pay attention and turned her chair to face the screen.

Moments later, Official Franklin's face popped up on the screen looking stressed and troubled. After a brief pause, he began to speak. "My friends, family, and fellow guildmates, I regret to inform you that the situation regarding the anti-hero organization has worsened dramatically."

Everyone looked at one another with concern. Whispers again filled the air before Sparrow snapped her fingers to silence them.

Franklin dabbed his forehead with a cloth and continued, "As many of you know, our goal was to hit them hard and fast, to stunt their growth before they gained too much momentum. But it seems we underestimated just how organized and influential they are."

Several images flashed on the screen of the group's handiwork. Acts of terrorism, secret meetings, monster conversions, the works. "We received a message from the leader of this organization. He refers to himself as the Purifier and warned that later today they will announce their presence to the world as well as leak sensitive information about the Heroes' Guild, information that could compromise its integrity and erode people's trust. We don't yet know what details they plan to announce or if they are truly able to do what they claim. Nevertheless, we need all guild and law enforcement officials to be ready to handle the possible panic that this could have on the public."

He took a very deep breath, held it for a moment, then exhaled. "All of you are to be commended for your dedication to protecting the people of this city. All guild leaders will be getting specified information on what to do for their districts if this threat materializes. This is Official Franklin saying thank you, and good luck to us all."

The message cut out and left the room in stunned silence. Static spoke first by asking, "What do we do now?"

Sparrow looked at her with unhidden panic. "We, um, we do what we were instructed. Or rather, what we will be instructed in the next message we get."

"So, what do we do until we get it?" Falcon asked

as he tapped his fingers on the table.

"Just, stay at the ready, uh, make sure all your gear is up to code and stuff..." Sparrow was mumbling. It was a habit she rarely displayed, and it only added to the uncertainty everyone was experiencing. Nobody moved from their chair. Her reply felt more like a floundering suggestion than it did an order.

"Well," James said, "you heard her. Let's stay on standby and prepare for our coming orders!" He was rallying everyone in hopes of taking some of the pressure off Sparrow. As the leader, everyone looked to her for direction, but she had none to give right now.

James waited for everyone else to file out of the room, then walked over to Sparrow, who was slumped over in her chair. "Can I do anything for you?" he asked empathetically.

She shook her head and sighed. "No, there really isn't anything you could do." She looked up at him and smiled. "Thank you for asking though."

He smiled back, warmly replying, "Anytime." Sitting on the table, he gave her shoulder a playful squeeze. "I know you're uncertain about what to do right now, but try not to worry. We will deal with it as it comes, just like you said."

She nodded and sniffled. "I know that, but I can't help but feel anxious. I hate when I don't have an answer for the people I care about." A tear formed and slid down her cheek.

"Hey, it's okay," James tenderly assured. "You

won't always know exactly what to say or do, but we all love and support you. We all know what an amazing guild leader you are. All anyone ever says about you is how you really show you care about us, how you inspire confidence, and how you always have our backs."

Her face began to soften as his words restored her self-esteem. "Really?" she asked.

"Really," he tenderly assured.

The next thing they knew they were staring into one another's eyes, fixated on their beauty. Slowly, their faces began to inch closer, their cheeks blushing as their noses brushed up against the other's. Just before their lips could meet, another notification appeared on the computer screen, letting out a ding and snapping them back to reality.

Realizing what almost happened, they jerked back and tried to save face. James cleared his throat and walked back to his chair. "So, I, uh, should probably go get the others or something, right?"

Sparrow hid her face behind one of her hands. "Yeah, uh-huh, that sounds like a good plan, go do that, thanks!"

James scurried out of the room with a beet-red face and a tingling stomach. Once he was gone, Sparrow lowered her head down on the desk and let out an embarrassed sigh.

Later that day, the foretold threat materialized. All the broadcasting systems, the radio stations, every possible means of communication were hijacked by the cultists.

As promised, the leader of the organization, the Purifier, sent out a grim warning: "The world is sick," he stated in a low, commanding voice. "The heroes you worship are nothing more than liars, empty vessels soaking up your adoration. They align themselves with the criminals of the world while claiming to fight for your safety. This is folly and deception. Rather than give your efforts to them, join our ranks, and aid us in the rebirth of this doomed, dying planet. We are called the Cleansers, and if you join us in our struggle, you will be guaranteed safety. If you resist us, then you will be left behind. Like the old ways of the world, you will be eliminated."

The transmission cut out, letting all normal broadcasts continue. With the police out in droves and heroes on every corner, most of the panic was kept to a minimum. Unfortunately, the damage was done. Dread and fear took hold of the populous and people splintered in their loyalties. If the Cleansers were hoping to spread panic, then they had accomplished their goal.

14/SECRETS

In the months that followed, the world braced for the impending attack. A surge of volunteers flocked to the guild while on the other side of the issue many began to support the Cleansers and their ideology.

James and his fellow guildmates kept more than busy trying to keep the bigger threats under control. Massive monster attacks became a daily occurrence, and their battles grew ever more intense, ripping up large swaths of the city and fostering contempt for the guild.

Ever since their close call in the guildhall, Sparrow began to assign James as her field partner with greater frequency. He suspected she was trying to spend more time with him while using work as a pretext. She always managed to come up with a flimsy excuse as to why they needed to team up, not that he was complaining. Despite Kazav's stern warnings not to get involved in a relationship, James found himself unable to pull his thoughts away from her.

With her defenses weakening and her affection for him growing, Sparrow decided she could no longer have any secrets between them. She was determined to tell him something shocking, something she had been holding in for years. A secret that only she and a handful of others knew. Once alone with James, she began to pace, unsure of how to bring it up.

His concern for her grew the longer she remained silent. Looking at the pain in her eyes, he felt compelled to ask, "Sparrow, what's going on? Are you okay?"

She looked back at him, fear streaked across her face. Then, with a flick of her wrist, she opened a black portal in the middle of the room. "Come with me," she commanded as she leaped into the rotating vortex, disappearing.

"Uh, okay?"

He hopped through the portal, unsure of what to expect. An endless, crimson-colored void stretched as far as the eye could see, a world of her own making. It was easy to become disoriented as there were no floors, walls, or landmarks of any kind. The only other thing in sight was Sparrow.

She stood in front of him, her hands covering her face. Then, with intense emotion, she spoke. "James, there is something I need to tell you, something awful."

He walked over and took her hand in his. "What's wrong?" he asked while wiping a tear from her cheek.

Sparrow released his hand and stepped back. Now with space between them, she looked into his eyes. Seeing the warmth and trust in them as they gazed back, she unleashed her awful secret, no longer able to hide it from the man she held so dear.

"James, the Heroes' Guild is not what it claims to be."

His eyes narrowed as confusion took hold. "What do you mean, Sparrow?"

Her heart fluttered. Even just saying what little she had was soul-crushing. That feeling, combined with the thought of breaking James' spirit, was almost too much to endure. Pushing the pain down, she continued with her awful revelation.

"The Heroes' Guild is nothing more than a puppet organization. It's a corrupt, dirty, unfaithful den of fake heroes and empty promises."

James started to laugh. He thought she was referring to all the insincere, wannabe fame hogs that he grew up despising. "I mean, yeah, there are a lot of bad apples out there," he replied as he stepped closer. "But I don't see why that's bothering you now? You knew that long before I did."

"No!" she cried out in frustration. "I'm not just talking about a few bad heroes. I'm talking about the entire organization. Top to bottom, it's all a carefully crafted lie!"

He was beginning to grasp what she had been trying to say. At first, he thought this was all a trial, or maybe a test to prove his loyalties. But Sparrow was dead serious, her tear-filled eyes and quivering lips dashing his theory to pieces. Once it sunk in, his legs turned to rubber, and he started to wobble. "Are you saying that HQ, the officials, all the top heroes, all of them are just...fake?"

She nodded, confirming the horrible truth and shattering his innocent reality. James slumped down and gripped his chest as a panic taking hold.

"But...why?"

She reached out and grabbed him before he collapsed. With his head in her arms, she explained the best she could. "Years ago, long before any of us had even been born, the Heroes Guild began to lose in its war against the villains." Stroking his hair, she continued, "They were faced with a choice. They could either keep fighting, right down to their inevitable end, or they could negotiate with their enemies to survive and maintain order in the world. They chose the latter."

He sat up, anger now replacing shock. "So, they sold themselves out in exchange for the guarantee not to be completely wiped out?"

Sparrow nodded rather than answered. It was so much easier than having to say the words aloud.

"But why? I just... I don't understand!" James slammed his fist onto the vaguely defined ground. Sparrow winced at his outburst, pained at the turmoil it was causing him. Then, a realization hit him. Sparrow knew of the truth...but how?

"How did you learn about all this?"

She placed her hand on his face in hopes of

calming him. She was willing to answer any question he had, anything to restore his trust. "Years back, when I was just a rising hero, I was like you. I had no idea of the dark truth behind the organization. Then, when I rose high enough in the rankings, I was offered a position in the top twenty."

"Top twenty?" James repeated. "I had no idea you made it that far."

"Nobody did. I never officially joined. You see, before you can join, you have to go through an initiation. One of the steps is being told the truth of the Guild and the reasons behind it. If you swear to keep it a secret from everyone, then, and only then, are you allowed to join."

James' eyes went wide. The fact that Sparrow made it that far and yet never became a member could only mean one thing. He looked at her, a smile breaking out on his once-sullen face. "You didn't accept the offer, did you?"

She shook her head. "No, I didn't. I was tempted but... I just knew I would never be able to enjoy it. Not while lying to the people that I love. I declined the offer and swore not to reveal the truth to anyone. If I did, they threatened to brand me as a traitor and deny all accusations."

A warmth grew in James, soothing his heart and mending the wound. After everything he had gone through, after everyone who had lied to him and let him down, Sparrow would always be Sparrow. He realized he didn't care about everything else. At that moment, all he could feel was pride, pride for the woman he cared for.

He propped up her face with his hand, sliding her cheek into his palm. "You amaze me, Sparrow," he murmured. "After everything you endured, all the blood and sweat you shed to achieve your dream, rather than be bought off, you took the high road. You are the kind of hero the world needs and the kind of person I admire with all my heart."

She began to smile, her cheeks turning a rosy red. "You certainly know how to flatter," she teased.

He laughed and hugged her tight. "I meant every word."

They sat there in the void, holding one another close. If it were up to James, he would have stayed like that forever, but Sparrow wanted to get back to the team. A crazy idea popped into her head, and she wanted to share it with everyone. Maybe, just maybe, the Heroes Guild could be redeemed.

They passed through the portal and watched it shut behind them, dispersing into the air like a puff of smoke fading into the night sky. Sparrow began to walk out of the room. She was eager to call the team to share with them what she had just revealed to James.

"Sparrow, wait!" James shouted just before she crossed the doorway. "There is one last thing I need to tell you, something very important."

"What is it?" she asked as he approached her, closing the gap between them.

Before she could process what was happening, he pulled her close and planted a kiss directly on her lips.

Sparrow had no idea how to react. Time was moving in slow motion, and she could see every single millisecond passing before her eyes. As he ended the kiss and pulled away, Sparrow stood there motionless, her eyes still open, her lips still pursed. James started worry that he had crossed a line, that maybe she didn't want him to do that.

"I'm sorry, Sparrow. I didn't mean to grab you like that. I just thought that maybe, I mean, it seemed like, well, that maybe you-"

Before he could finish his apology, she grabbed his face and kissed him right back.

Now James was the one in shock. "Wow," he whispered as Sparrow pulled away. Then, with a wink and a smile, she left the room.

Later that day, Sparrow called for a meeting. She was determined to tell the entire team the truth. By the time she finished, there was nothing but anger, pain, and feelings of betrayal running wild.

Owl was so distraught he let off a sonic scream, blasting a hole through the roof. Static became so emotional that she glowed, sending out arcs of electricity that nearly melted her chair. Hawk and Falcon argued over who could breakdance the best, splitting off from the matter at hand and causing unnecessary drama.

Sparrow and James tried to keep things under control the best they could but had trouble focusing. Both kept sneaking furtive looks at one another, turning away in a blush when they caught the other staring.

After calming everyone down, Sparrow started her pitch. "I know this was a lot to take in," she said from the head of the table. "But this is not the end. We don't have to live with this sad reality if we choose not to."

"What other choice do we have?" Static pleaded through tears and snot. "The Heroes' Guild is the only thing we've ever known!"

Sparrow looked out at the table, a clever grin growing on her face. "You're right, the Heroes Guild is the only organization most of us have ever known. They are powerful, established, and very influential. But there's one thing they aren't: honest."

"What do you propose we do?" Owl asked, unsure of the point she was making. "You don't intend for us to fight against the Guild, do you?"

She shook her head. "No, what I'm proposing is we start our own."

Everyone became silent as they shared insecure glances with one another, wondering who would speak first.

James decided to jumpstart things with a rousing speech. "I know this is scary, and you may feel confused as to whom you can trust. The truth is I'm sacred too. But with Sparrow, we have never had to question if she cares. She always lets us know. We never have to wonder if she has our back – she always does. Even if I have lost faith in the Guild, I know I will never lose my trust in her." Standing up, he looked her in the eyes and said, "I'm with you, Sparrow."

One by one, the other heroes rose as they made their choice.

"Me too," Static chirped. "I trust you, mind, heart, and soul!"

Hawk and Falcon nodded and rose from their chairs. "You can count us in."

Owl put down the comic book he was engrossed in and faced Sparrow. "To the grave and beyond, you have my allegiance."

"Well, all right, then!" Sparrow said, her heart swelling with warmth. "Get some rest, everyone, because first thing tomorrow we will begin hashing out the details of our brand-new guild!"

The room erupted in joyous shouting as excitement and hope came alive. After a brief back and forth of ideas for the new guild, everyone filed out and went to bed.

James, on the other hand, was finding it impossible to close his eyes as images of him and Sparrow replayed in his head. He was so glad he took that risk, so glad he manned up and kissed her. Everything felt like it was coming together, like his life finally had a purpose.

Then, breaking the silence of his dark bedroom, Kazav said, *"That was...a very interesting day."* James' *flinched at the sound of his voice. For a moment he had almost forgotten about him.* "You know those big corporations your planet seems to be fond of, James?"

James could tell Kazav was about to launch into a prolonged vent and decided to humor him rather than avoid it. *"Yeah, what about them?"*

Kazav snickered, his voice taking on an increasingly demeaning tone. *"The Heroes Guild was no different. I mean, they had a corporate HQ! No place that has something called HQ is ever going to be anything more than a soul-sucking money pit. All organizations are destined to fail, not that I'm trying to cast doubt on your new and improved Heroes Guild idea."*

James was getting upset. He could handle Kazav's snarky comments and sarcastic attitude but now felt he was crossing a line. *"What makes you so sure?"* James challenged.

"I'm glad you asked, kid. You see, eventually your new guild will devolve into the old guild. Just like a corporation, as things grow, the process becomes more streamlined, and people begin to join for the wrong reasons. Things will fall apart for your guild the same way it did for this one."

"Well, I think you're wrong," James stated defensively. *"If you ask me, the only reason the current Heroes Guild failed was that they aligned themselves with the villains instead of keeping their integrity."*

There was a pause as Kazav processed what James had said. Then, in a serious and no-nonsense tone, he stated, *"I think we need to break into HQ."*

James fought back a restrained snort as he tried not to laugh. *"Break into HQ? Oh, so no biggie. I'll just bust into the most sacred and secure location on the planet."*

"Hold on, kid, just hear me out. What you just said got me thinking, what if the Heroes Guild and the Cleansers are in cahoots?"

"Uh, that seems like a bit of a stretch, Kazav. What motive could they possibly have for working together?"

"Just think about it. The Heroes Guild has deals with all the major crime syndicates and allows them to operate unimpeded so long as they don't make too much trouble, right?"

James nodded. *"Right..."*

"Well, doesn't it seem likely that they would be extending the same kind of offer to this new threat?"

"I guess I could see that, but what would they gain? The Cleansers want to bring everyone down, not just the Heroes Guild. Do you think they would be willing to settle for less?"

"I don't think they're a separate organization. I think they're one and the same."

"Huh...What makes you think there's such a strong connection?" James asked, growing increasingly convinced of the possibility.

Kazav sighed. *"I don't know yet, but I think the*

proof is in HQ."

"Look, Kazav, your gut, it's almost never wrong, so I am willing to play devil's advocate. Let's say that what you're suggesting is true. How would we even go about breaking in? We don't even know where HQ is!"

Kazav let out a naughty chuckle. *"You're right, kid, you don't know where it is, but I do."*

"Seriously? How do you know that?"

"Remember when we teleported to its secret location? A normal human would never have been able to see what's beyond the walls of that cold metal prison. But I'm not human, remember? I knew exactly where we were."

James let out an impressed, *"Wow."* He was growing more intrigued by the second. *"Okay, fine, let's say I'm on board with this crazy idea. How would we not get caught? We can't exactly go traipsing around out in the open."*

Kazav buzzed with excitement. *"Let me show you."*

Right after Kazav finished speaking, James glowed, his skin turning a vibrant mix of red and black as he became enveloped in a cocoon of dark, oozing energy. A loud crack thundered through the room as a flash of light singed the bedding James was resting on. No sooner did the light flash that James completely disappeared.

"What the..." James remarked as he looked down at where his feet used to be.

"Pretty cool, right?" Kazav asked excitedly.

"Am I invisible?"

"You sure are, kiddo."

He tried to find his hands and felt around on the bed. All he could see was the impression his fingers made against the mattress. *"How did you do this, Kazav?"*

"Ah ah ah," he teased. *"A magician never reveals his secrets."*

"Is there any way you could make it so I can still see myself?" James asked after stubbing his toe on every corner in the room.

"Hmm, let me see what I can do."

Slowly, James phased into sight. It wasn't crystal clear, but he could at least determine where his feet and arms were.

"So, kid, you ready to break into HQ?"

James grinned. The very thought was both terrifying and exhilarating.

"Yeah, let's break into HQ!"

15/B&E

They slipped out into the night, careful not to wake the team. According to Kazav, HQ was thousands of miles away. Now able to leap thousands of feet at a time, the distance proved to be a minor obstacle for James. It was a serene experience as he flew over the forests, lakes, and rivers that dotted the landscape below. Cool night air flowed through his hair, bringing with it the sweet smell of night blossoms. Such a therapeutic atmosphere helped to calm his nerves for the task ahead.

"Once we get there, how do we get in?" he asked Kazav, his anxiety rising.

"I'm not entirely sure. We'll have to figure that out when we arrive."

A short time later, they arrived at the location Kazav felt was accurate. "Are you sure about this?" James asked aloud, his voice echoing in the dusty air. With nothing but tumbleweeds and parched, arid grassland for miles, it seemed like a mistake.

"I'm sure! Just keep looking. I can sense it here, somewhere."

James launched off the ground and shot up into the sky. From his new vantage, he could see for miles around. The only thing that caught his attention was a flickering light coming from what looked to be a run-down gas station. "That can't be it, right?"

"Only one way to find out!" Kazav remarked enthusiastically.

Once they arrived, it became clear that nobody had been in there for a long time. "Looks like a dead end," James mumbled sullenly.

"Not so fast, kid! Take another look behind the counter."

Jumping behind the plastic countertop, James examined it top to bottom. On the underside of the counter was a secret button. "Wow! How did you know that would be there?"

Kazav let out a cool chuckle. *"It was a lucky guess. Once you get to be my age, your instincts become very acute."*

James clicked the button, causing a cranking noise to emanate from the center of the room. The floor tiles parted and folded inwards, revealing a cobweb-infested secret entrance.

"Bingo!" Kazav exclaimed.

With great unease, James entered the tunnel, wiping cobwebs from his hair as he descended. *"It doesn't seem like anyone has used this tunnel for a long time,"* Kazav stated.

James nodded, hoping what Kazav said was true. "Hopefully it doesn't raise any alarms."

"Relax, kid, you're invisible. Even if they have an

army of cameras, they won't be able to see you!"

"Well, I've never been invisible before. It's very easy to forget."

They reached the bottom of the stairwell and passed through a metal hatch. On the other side was a concrete bunker full of old tech and equipment. As they looked through the rooms that branched off from the main walkway, James took the time to admire the countless posters and awards that still hung from the walls. *"This must have been HQ's living space when they first got their start,"* he observed.

The rooms looked like they belonged to low-level heroes as they had few accommodations. Their setup was all the same: an old metal bed frame with a few chairs and a table. Some rooms had a stand for armor but most of them were very basic.

They kept moving and got to the end of the hall-way, stopping at a large metal blast door that hindered their advance. James tried to open it using the rusted metal lock but only managed to snap it off.

"What now?"

"Knock it down!" Kazav commanded.

"Are you sure? It feels like that might make too much noise." James powered up his fist and pressed it against the door. *"How about this instead?"* With his powers, he melted a hole in the door, turning it into a molten puddle of slag.

"Nice thinking, kid! Now, onward!"

They stepped into a much more luxurious environment. This was obviously reserved for the high-level heroes. It looked like a mix between a hotel lounge and a corporate building complex.

James frowned while looking through the fancy, high-tech living quarters. He felt like this was part of the problem with the Guild. The second they started separating people into classes they became divided.

He walked as he mused, reaching yet another stairwell. James opted to jump down rather than spend time walking. He landed with a thud as the force of his descent sent cracks crawling through the floor.

"Oops."

"Maybe try sneaking around in a way that doesn't let them know you're here?" Kazav scolded. Then, looking ahead at a modern, sleek metal door, he announced, *"I think this is it!"*

James pressed his hands to the door and tried burning a hole through it like last time, but it absorbed the heat like a space tile. Trying a new approach, he emitted a concentrated beam of energy, slicing through the door like a laser cutter. Behind the blast door was a storage closet devoid of human activity. It was empty besides a few boxes of old tech stacked up in the corners.

"And we are in," Kazav whispered excitedly.

"Yeah, but where do we go from here?"

Kazav felt things out while James made his way

through the room. With a handle on what direction to move, he advised, *"We need to go down. Try and find an elevator or something."*

James exited the storage room and darted through the never-ending hallways as he tried to remain silent. Not being able to be seen was a huge advantage, but he was still being as cautious as possible. There were a lot of heroes wandering around, some of which he figured might have the power to detect him.

After a few minutes of exploration, he found an elevator and clicked the down button. The lights above the door lit up as it approached his level, counting down until it came to a slow stop. His heart almost exploded once the doors parted, and he found himself standing directly in front of Official Franklin.

Kazav could tell James was freaking out and rushed to calm him. *"Chill out, kid, you're invisible. He can't see you, so just hold still and don't panic!"*

Franklin looked around to see why the elevator had stopped. He looked right, then left. Shrugging, he closed the doors and continued his descent.

James let out a relieved sigh as he clicked the down button again, this time for a different door.

"What are you so tense for? Nobody can see you, remember?"

"I know I'm invisible, Kazav! I'm just not used to it yet."

"Okay, okay, calm down, kid, yeesh. Try not to panic is all I'm saying."

The elevator stopped on a floor above the one he wanted, indicating that someone else was about to get on.

Uh-oh! James said internally. He suspended himself close to the ceiling by pressing his hands and legs against the sides of the elevator, a move he took from a spy movie. The doors opened and a cluster of office workers huddled in.

"Good thinking, kid. There are way too many people all smushed together. You would have been made for sure!"

James listened in as the workers talked among themselves, revealing juicy tidbits of information.

"You hear about the massive number of people defecting to the Cleansers?" one worker asked another.

A young woman in a business suit replied, "Yeah, they aren't letting the public know, but they have way more support than anyone is letting on. You know, trying to keep panic to a minimum."

Another worker laughed and patted her on the shoulder. "Isn't it funny how quickly humans will start turning on one another when they are afraid? It's pretty embarrassing."

They all chuckled until the elevator doors opened and they stepped off. James jumped down when they left and pressed the button for the doors to close.

Kazav laughed. *"As sad as that was to hear, it is*

kinda true."

"It's also equally true that adversity brings people together," James retorted.

Kazav let out an unconvinced, *"Meh,"* and left it at that.

Now on the floor they desired, James snuck out into the hallway and waited for Kazav's instruction.

"Wait!" Kazav shouted as they passed the door to a private office.

"What? What is it?"

"This is it, kid, this is the room we need!"

James checked out the entrance. It was a normal-looking door with no real security. Hardly a door he would have expected a horrible secret to be kept behind.

"Are you sure?"

"Yup! I'm sure. My instincts are screaming at me to look inside!"

James jiggled the handle. The door was locked but had no security system attached. He tore the handle off and entered the office. It was a quaint setup with nothing out of the ordinary. There were a few knickknacks on the table and a bookshelf full of various kinds of reading material standing behind the desk, but Kazav felt no pull toward them. The only interesting item in the entire room was a laptop sitting closed on the desk. The computer was bolted down in a titanium casing, making it almost impossible to remove.

"That's it, right there!" Kazav announced, his voice vibrating with excitement.

James opened the computer but was blocked by a screen asking for a password.

"Now what?"

"Hmm, well, it looks like the keys that have the most erosion on them are the L, E, R, C, N, S, and A keys. Let's try and see what words we can create using those options."

James thought long and hard about what words he could make. It made him feel dumb, but he was at a loss. *"I'm blanking, Kazav, I can't think of any valid word that contains those letters.*

"Hmm, try lancers."

James entered the word into the box. "Password incorrect," the computer informed him.

"Uhm, try rencals?

He typed it in only to once again be denied. *"Nope, it says incorrect and that we have one last attempt before we are locked out."*

Kazav came to a startling realization. *"Wait, I'm not considering he may be using the same key more than once."* He let out a concerned sigh and said, *"Try the word, Cleansers."*

James hesitated. *"Are you sure?"*

"I hope not."

He clicked in the keys and hit enter. The computer screen said, "Welcome," and booted up.

James got a bad feeling in the pit of his stomach. *"Well, that's not good. The Cleansers may have breached HQ!"*

Once the computer booted up, a ton of windows flooded the screen. James scrolled through the computer's files as he looked for any signs of malfeasance. After a half-hour of looking, he failed to find anything substantial.

Kazav chimed in with a suggestion. *"Try typing in a keyword. Maybe something like Cleanser or something along those lines."*

James typed in the word *Cleanser*. Clicking enter, a lone result remained in the inbox.

"This has got to be it!"

It required another password, but using his previous method, Kazav cracked it in no time.

James now had access to the contents of the message and Kazav read it aloud. *"Greetings, fellow titans of power,"* the email was titled. He then read the body. *"The Heroes Guild recognizes the threat you present to the world order. As agreed in previous communications, we will allow you to seize the sectors of your choosing so long as you advance no further. You will have total control over what happens to these allotments of land so long as no further aggression is displayed."*

"This is disgusting!" James cried out. *"They're playing chess with these people's lives. Treating them like pawns they can move or toss away."* He found a flash drive sitting on the desk and uploaded the informa-

tion.

With the evidence in hand, he headed for the elevator. As he waited for it to reach his level, a voice rang out through the halls. A familiar voice, one that sent chills down his spine.

"Is that Jeremy? Oh man, this is bad! This is so very bad!"

"Relax, kid, relax, they won't be able to see you."

"Yeah, but what if they can sense me?"

"Just shut up and be quiet! They won't sense you if you don't move!"

James hid in the corner as his brother, along with several other high-ranking heroes, walked past the elevators. James eavesdropped on their conversation.

"So, you all know the plan, right?" Jeremy asked the rest of the group.

"Yup!" the Crimson Lady replied. "Fight them until sectors F and G fall and then pull back and let them have it."

An official interjected. His face was contorted from concern. "But what about the citizens living in those sectors – what happens to them?"

Jeremy stared him down, displeased with his interruption. "It's an unfortunate sacrifice, but one we have to make. Don't go soft on me now. We have some difficult choices to make, but someone has to make them."

Their voices trailed off as they moved further

away. Once he felt it was safe to move, James made his way back to the elevator doors and clicked the up button. They backtracked and made it back into the tunnels they entered from under the assumption that everyone was none the wiser.

Once outside, James leaped out into the distance, his heart set on making it back home as fast as possible. It seemed they got away without anyone detecting them, and James was about to let out a laugh from all the adrenaline coursing through his body.

That was, until excruciating pain erupted in his back, sending him crashing into the forest below.

He looked up from the crater he lay in to see none other than Jeremy hovering above him, a hostile scowl beaming from his eyes. "You wouldn't leave without saying hi to your big brother, would you, James?"

16/BROTHERLY DISAGREEMENT

The serene forest, full of babbling brooks and peaceful gullies was quickly turned into a cracked and cratered battle zone as James and his brother squared off.

"I don't want to fight you," James said.

Jeremy ignored his pleas for peace, instead sending out a barrage of lethal punches. "Then you shouldn't have stuck your nose where it didn't belong!"

James dodged and deflected the blows with impressive skill but was still no match for the titan chasing after him. Another bone-shattering blow sent him zipping through the air, sonic booms travelling through the forest. He came to rest in the side of a mountain after the impact tore a chunk of it from its base and down into the forest below. Jeremy now hovered in front of him with a cold, emotionless gaze.

"I'm amazed at your progress, little bro. You've come a long way in a short period. It's...suspicious." He descended onto the ledge next to James and asked,

"What could have possibly motivated you to break into HQ? Are you working with the Cleansers now?"

James scowled. "No, but I'd say it's safe to say that you are."

"That's preposterous. Why would you think that?"

He freed himself from the cliff wall and walked over to Jeremy. "I heard you talking about how the Guild is just going to let those lunatics take over parts of the city! What about the people living there? What is going to happen when a war breaks out on their doorstep? "

Jeremy's face grew sullen, almost remorseful. "I see. I'm sorry you had to hear that."

"How could you betray the people you swore to protect?"

Jeremy shook his head at James' outburst. He was amused by what he perceived as a lack of common sense. "You think it's that simple, do you? Wow, you truly are adorably simple." Then, grabbing James by the collar, he shot up into the sky. They flew toward the city, stopping once they reached the center. "You see all these people, James? Every single one of them gets to wake up, go to work, live their life, because they don't know the truth."

James tried prying Jeremy's hand off him. "Yeah, that's the problem. Instead of telling them the truth, you just continue to lie to them and now you dug yourselves in too deep! Now the only way forward is by resetting the bone of the leg you broke."

"Your sense of self-righteousness is cute, but if there was any other way to keep most of the city safe, don't you think we would have changed course already? A small number may have to be sacrificed, but that's life. Is that so hard for you to understand?"

"Oh, please," James snorted doubtfully. "You wouldn't change things if you could. The only reason you became a hero was to bask in the glory of the people you think are beneath you."

"And you think you are any better? Do you think that intention alone defines what it means to be a good hero? Well, guess what? Intentions don't keep people safe; they don't bring results."

"You're right, they don't. But at least they show what's in your heart. They show what you fight for and give your battles real meaning!"

Jeremy chuckled as he descended closer to the city. "A very cute sentiment, but naive." Then, setting James down on a rooftop, he asked, "So what now? Are you going to go back to your little clubhouse and tell all your friends the truth?"

James shook his head and grinned. "They already know the truth."

"Oh, so Sparrow told you, huh? I knew we shouldn't have let her leave. I knew she would just cause problems."

James tightened his fist. "Don't you dare threaten her!"

Jeremy raised an eyebrow. "Well, well, well, looks like you got a little crush, don't ya, bro?"

Then, so fast James couldn't react, Jeremy shot forward and grabbed his collar. "Let me explain what happens now. If you say anything to the public, then I'll have you and all your little friends labeled as traitors. That means you get hunted down and thrown in detainment for the rest of your life, and that's if you're lucky."

"Is that a promise?" James asked, a cocky smirk growing.

Jeremy didn't reply. He just let go of his collar, grinned, and blasted off back to HQ.

Kazav shuddered. *"You should get back to the Guild before he changes his mind about letting you go."*

"Yeah, they need to know what's happening. They might be mad I went out on my own, but hopefully they will understand."

Once back at the guild hall, James woke the team. Now all together, he brought them up to speed.

Sparrow ran her fingers through her hair. "This is so, so, bad!"

Owl shook his head. "It's so much worse than we thought it to be."

With his feet up on the table, Falcon declared, "Pshhh, I ain't afraid of no corrupt heroes. Bring 'em all on right now. I'll take 'em all out!"

Hawk smacked the back of his head. "Yeah, right, like you could take down the top twenty."

"Well, I bet I could," Falcon mumbled, trailing off until silent.

"What happens now?" Super Static asked Sparrow, her bright blue eyes squinting with concern.

James slapped the table and said, "We stay the course. All this proves is how badly we need a new guild. One that won't stoop to such awful lows."

Sparrow nodded, adding, "James is right. All this new info tells us is how badly we need to change things once this all blows over. We stick to our current plan and worry about dealing with the Heroes Guild later. Since we're all gathered, this seems like a good time to start planning the logistics of how our new organization will operate."

The meeting lasted well into the night, a back and forth of suggestions and revisions concluding with a set of rough rules. Each day they tweaked things further until, finally, they felt they had reached a consensus.

While most of the team's sprits were high, James was growing increasingly frustrated. The guilt of putting his friends in danger was tearing at his conscience. Sparrow sensed something was wrong and was eager to confront him.

"Hey, handsome," she teased as she walked into the kitchen.

"What's cooking, good-looking?" he replied with a smile.

"Everything okay?" Sparrow asked as James

swirled his food around on his plate. "I know we haven't been able to spend as much time together recently. I hope that's not what's been bothering you.

"No, it's nothing like that," he reassured. "I'm just worried about all of you. Maybe it was a mistake to do what I did, breaking into HQ."

Sparrow sat next to him and held his hand. "Well, I don't think it was a mistake, if it makes you feel better."

"Thanks, that's sweet of you to say." He pushed his plate away, adding, "I still think it would have been better had I not."

Sparrow scooted closer and patted his back. "Had you not, we would have never known just how deep the corruption goes," she stated, trying to console him.

"Yeah, I guess you're right. I just hate the idea of having put you all in danger."

Sparrow gently nudged his face closer to hers. "No matter what happens, I will always have your back. Never forget that"

She gave him a gentle kiss and rested her head against his. He kissed her forehead and held her tight. It was moments like this that made him forget all his troubles.

Super Static walked in to get an apple from the fridge and noticed the two of them having a moment. "Don't mind me," she teased. "Just getting an apple, and then you two lovebirds can go back to smooching or whatever else it is you were doing."

James and Sparrow chuckled awkwardly as Static left. "Well," Sparrow remarked, " I need to get back to work anyway. I just wanted to check in with you and make sure you were okay."

He blushed. A fuzzy, warm feeling enveloped his body. "Thank you, it means a lot that you care so much."

Sparrow blushed and gave him a little wink as she left the room.

Later, when James was alone, Kazav decided now would be a good time to ask him a personal question. One that he had been waiting to ask for a while.

"Is it love?"

"Huh?" James replied. *"Is what love?"*

"What you and Sparrow have, is it love?"

James was caught off guard. *"Oh, uh, well, what if it is?"*

"There is nothing wrong with it. I just don't want you to become distracted. Love can make people do stupid things."

James chuckled and asked, *"You speak from experience, don't you?"*

"That was a low blow," Kazav mumbled.

"I'm sorry. I didn't mean to upset you."

"Just stay the course is all I'm saying. Things are about to get insane, and you gotta have zero distractions if you are going to succeed in changing the world."

"Thanks, Kazav, I'll be careful."

James leaned back in his chair and reminisced about their first meeting. Just him alone in his room until a freaky shadow guy popped out of nowhere and, rather than eat him alive like he thought, covered his foot with a blanket. Despite his aloof and distant attitude, James felt Kazav really did care about him in more than just a host-parasite way.

"I trust you," James spoke into the room.

Kazav couldn't tell if he was talking to him or not. *"What's that, kid?"*

"Do you remember how before I said I couldn't trust someone who wouldn't tell me all about themselves?"

"Yeah?"

"Well, I trust you," James repeated.

"Oh, uh, well, I trust you too, kid."

James smiled and felt a peace he had not known for a long time. Even though the Guild might have been untrue about who it was, he knew that if he had Sparrow, Kazav, and the rest of the team by his side, then there was nothing to fear.

17/ IT BEGINS

Empty streets and an eerie silence – these were the sights and sounds that permeated the city as the day of reckoning arrived. The Cleansers made their move and amassed their forces outside the city limits, biding their time and waiting for the best moment to strike.

In defensive positions, the team awaited the coming battle, grouped together as they awaited the first shot. Knowing the truth of the war, James and the rest of the team had come to a decision. If HQ called for a ceasefire, then they would simply ignore it. They would let everyone know the truth of the matter and fight the Cleansers down to the very end.

All the various guild chapters had every member positioned throughout the city awaiting the main attack. Law enforcement was out in droves patrolling the streets. All citizens had been evacuated to special shelters far outside the city or had been instructed to shelter in their homes. Hours ticked by without any action, and the heroes were starting to get tense.

"This is bogus!" Falcon griped.

"Yeah!" Hawk added. "What are they making us wait for? Are they too scared?"

"It could be a tactic to elicit fear," Owl remarked as he sat on a bench, flipping through a magazine labeled *Clever Feather*.

Sparrow and James sat by one another and tried to keep calm. "It's going to be okay," she reassured as he bounced his leg like a maniac.

"It's not the battle I'm concerned about. It's everything we have to accomplish after the battle that is worrying me."

She reached out for his hand. "One thing at a time. We will cross that bridge when we get there."

He gripped her hand back and smiled. Somehow, she always managed to calm him. He found her voice to be a soothing, angelic balm to whatever fear took hold in his soul. A few minutes later, they began to hear chatter on the radios. It sounded like some of the other sectors were starting to see some action. The tension only grew as they stood by for further instruction. Their initial orders were to stay in their sector and not leave unless commanded by HQ, but it was hard to wait around while your fellow guildmates were overrun by monsters.

Sector after sector saw an influx of Cleanser combatants, adding to the frustration everyone was experiencing. In no time, the fighting became close enough for them to hear. Growls, roars, screams, and shots rang out into the air and sent anxious shivers down everyone's spine.

Then, over the com of a nearby officer, they

heard the words: "Unidentified combatant entering the sector. Repeat. Unidentified combatant entering the sector."

Everyone braced for what they felt was the start of their own battle. Instead, they were greeted by a man with his hands above his head slowly walking towards the heroes.

"Easy, buddy, easy," the officer next to them shouted. "This is an active battle zone. What are you doing out here?"

The man approached the heroes and started to speak. "I'm here to turn myself in," the man announced with a quivering voice.

James was weary. He wanted to be sure this wasn't a trap. "What do you mean, turn yourself in? Are you a Cleanser?"

The man nodded. "I was, but I don't want to do this anymore! I'm scared."

The officer frisked him for weapons and then handcuffed him to a chair.

They all decided to question him for information. If he was telling the truth, then he could be an invaluable asset.

James started to put the screws to him. "If you want your safety to be guaranteed, then we are gonna need some information."

The man nodded and asked, "What do you want to know?"

James did a chair turn and flipped it backwards.

He didn't really know how to interrogate someone, but he had watched plenty of crime shows on TV and figured he would just imitate what he saw the best he could.

"What's the battle plan? How many people do you have in your little club? Who are you working with? We want to know it all, so start talking!"

The man's face became pained. "I can't tell you that."

James let out a laugh. "Well, champ, you gotta tell us something! Otherwise, why turn yourself over in the first place?"

The man shook his head. "No, I mean, I won't tell you any of that. If they found out that I was the one who ruined their plans, they would kill me!"

Sparrow slid over next to James and formed a shadow dagger in her hands. "They might kill you if you speak, huh? Well, if you don't, then I'll make sure you wish they had!"

James looked over at Sparrow alarmedly. He knew she was bluffing, but she sounded way too believable. The man thought about it as he stared at the pulsating ebony blade protruding from Sparrow's hand.

"Okay, okay, fine." He let out a massive sigh and spilled the beans. "The entire battle is a diversion."

James moved closer, an intimidating look plastered on his face. "What? What do you mean, a diversion?"

The man chuckled as he stared into his eyes. "This is so much bigger than any of you know. The battle is just a diversion to keep the heroes busy. The real goal has always been getting to the Nexus Orb."

Sparrow locked her gaze on him. "What! They know where it is?"

The man nodded affirmatively.

She grabbed his collar and pulled him close. "Where is it?"

"I don't know where it is, exactly, but I know where they're looking."

"Tell us!" Sparrow demanded as she brought the blade closer.

The man swallowed nervously and said, "Outside the city to the east is a quarry. They seem to believe it's somewhere around there. But I swear that's all I know!"

Sparrow retracted the dagger and started giving commands. "Static, Hawk, Falcon, and Owl, you all stay here and defend this sector. James, you and I are going to this quarry and stopping them before they find what they're looking for."

"Yes, ma'am!" the group replied.

Sparrow and James took off in the direction the hostage had given them. They found the quarry and hid behind some bushes while they scoped it out. The land around it had been completely leveled by massive machines. Monstrously large equipment was banging and drilling into the ground in and around the quarry, sending heaps of stone flying out into the air. James looked through the shrubbery and out at the massive piles of gravel piling up beside the machines. "It looks like they're digging further down. Maybe the Nexus Orb is buried under the quarry?"

Sparrow let out an agitated grunt. "Wherever it is, we have to stop them! If they get their hands on it, the entire world will fall!"

Before they could reach the mining equipment, they were halted by an army of mutated monsters just like the one James and Owl battled in the junk-yard. The creatures scattered in all directions to flank them, but Sparrow and James had little trouble dispatching them. By now, James had become an expert at using his plasma attacks to vaporized monster after monster while Sparrow had protected herself in full shadow armor and donned an energy blade that cut through the beasts like butter.

They moved together in perfect grace and harmony, defending the other from attacks and effortlessly complementing the other's moves and tactics. They both grinned as they sliced and burned through the hordes of monsters together in what almost felt like a dance.

The issue was less about the monster's strength and more about their numbers. The creatures just kept coming in ever-growing waves and made it impossible for them to advance.

"Enough of this!" James declared. "Sparrow, can you cover me for a few minutes?"

She finished sundering a monster in two and replied, "A few minutes? I think I can manage that!" She gave him an affirmative wink and got back to slicing.

James charged up for the most powerful plasma attack he had ever attempted. *"Kazav, give me everything you got."*

He planned to turn the entire quarry into a crater and end every threat all at once, but he needed time. He knelt on the ground and focused with all his might. Every bit of energy, every strand of strength, he mustered it all into a ball of pulsing and electrifying plasma that formed above him, growing larger with every passing second.

Sparrow was fending the monsters off with a masterful display of her powers. She twirled and flipped about, keeping the perimeter tight. One of the monsters reached out for James, but she intercepted it and kicked it so hard it flew into the sky without ever falling back down.

James began to glow and shimmer as the power flowed through him. Bolts of electricity struck several of the monsters attacking Sparrow, turning them into dust.

Once the Cleanser foot soldiers saw what James was doing, they joined the assault. Some of them fired weapons while others had powers and hurled fireballs, energy beams, and jagged shards at James from their hands. Once the projectiles reached him, they stopped mid-air, disintegrated, and only served to add to the power of his attack.

Sparrow had to step back as the ball grew and turned the ground around James into a puddle of molten goo. Once he couldn't charge it any further, James leaped up into the sky and, like an asteroid falling, released the burning plasma onto the ground below.

Sparrow had already evacuated to a safe distance before the ball turned everything into a bubbling pile of lava-like liquid. James fell back down to the ground, drained. Sparrow ran out to meet him, grabbing hold of him before he collapsed.

"Wow, James," she exclaimed in complete amazement. "That was incredible."

He smiled and gave her a wink, returning the one she gave him earlier. The victory was short-lived as something landed on the ground in front of them, pulling their attention away from one another. Sparrow set James' head down gently and got into a defensive position. No matter what it was, she was ready to protect James at any cost.

"Yes," a voice called out from behind the clouds of dust. "That was very impressive."

James winced; he knew exactly who it was.

Jeremy walked out from behind the screen of dirt and into full view.

Sparrow tensed up as he casually stepped closer, a sinister smile sown onto his face. He broke into a slow clap while giving out an ominous warning. "I'm afraid your little game ends here."

"Don't come one step closer," Sparrow ordered

Jeremy, who was now just an arm's length away. She held out a shadow blade in his direction to keep him at a distance.

Jeremy chuckled and grabbed hold of the pointed end of it. The blade had no effect, and he let his hand simmer in the dark energy to show her how powerless she was against him.

"How adorable that you have your girlfriend here to fight your battles, little bro."

Sparrow snarled at him, like a wolf showing its teeth before it bit. "So, what now? Are you here to stop us from keeping the world safe from the monsters you have aligned yourself with?"

"You think I'm going to believe anything you two say to me? I think it's more than clear that you're the ones with ill intentions."

"Liar!" she shouted while inching closer, her blade pointed at his heart.

Jeremy shook his head. "Enough. I don't have time for this. Since both of you are here, it's clear that you deduced the location of the Nexus Orb. But if you think for even one second that I'll let either one of you get your hands on it, then you are dead wrong."

Sparrow and James looked at one another, then back at Jeremy. "We don't know where it is," she attempted to explain.

Jeremy cut her off. "It doesn't matter. Either way, I'm not going to let you hold the world hostage with the Orb's powers. It's clear to me it's no longer safe in its current location, so I'll be recovering it for safekeeping."

His eyes glowed a bright and blinding red. Moments later, a high-powered laser beam erupted from them, flowing into the ground below. A massive hole formed, extending down for countless miles. The laser stream cut off, and Jeremy flew down into the molten tube he had created.

James looked over to Sparrow. "What just happened?"

She shrugged. "I have no clue! What do you think he plans to do with the Orb?"

James peered down into the hole. A faint orange glow shimmered from its depths, like a furnace sending light out into the dim night sky.

Kazav chimed in, a sullen tone in his voice. *"James, there's something I've been wanting to warn you about. I just wasn't sure how to bring it up."*

"Really? What is it, Kazav? Does it have something to do with the Orb?"

"Actually, it has something to do with your brother. You see, kid, I've been worried about Jeremy ever since we first encountered him. I got a dark and sinister vibe from him as he always gave off an inhuman quality. I could never pinpoint why until now."

"What is it?"

Kazav let out a sigh. *"It's because I don't think he's a human."*

"That's impossible," James remarked while shak-

ing his head. *"I grew up with him. My parents would have said something to me. He would have said something to me! How in the world could he not be human?"*

"Maybe they didn't know? Memories can be manipulated quite easily if one knows how to do it. An alien of superior power would have no trouble with such a trivial task."

"But that makes no sense!" James cried. *"Sure, he is incredibly powerful even by a hero's standards, but that's hardly a reason to suspect he's an imposter."*

"I'm not saying that it's true. All I'm saying is if it is true, it could explain why I don't pick up the typical energy waves from him that I should. All humans share a signature pattern in their life force that I can detect. When I look at Jeremy, I don't see one." Kazav continued to theorize as James searched his past for answers. *"Maybe that's why all of a sudden Jeremy's behavior changed all those years ago. It could be why his power and personality became so different so abruptly."*

James didn't know what to think. He remembered loving his brother so much and then losing him to his own pride and greed. He almost wanted to believe what was being said. At least then it would be a way to justify the years of pain and isolation he felt after that fateful day.

Sparrow didn't know what was happening to James. She could only wonder as he seemed to trail off into deep thought. It was as if he was conversing with someone.

"James," she called out. "Are you okay?"

He shook his head and looked back at her, or rather through her. His focus was blurred, and his vision was in a daze.

"Look, kid, I didn't mean to upset you. I just felt like now more than ever you needed to be confronted with the possibility."

James shook his head to try and refocus. He still didn't know what to think, but he was willing to trust Kazav and figure things out later. There were far more pressing matters to attend to.

"So, what do we do now?"

"Well," Kazav replied hesitantly. *"I think we need to go in after him. Maybe we can beat him to the Orb and keep him from doing whatever it is he's planning on doing with it?"*

James looked over into the endless abyss. *"You mean, down there?"*

"Yup"

James nodded begrudgingly and then turned to Sparrow. He brought one of his hands up to her face and caressed her cheek with his thumb. "Sparrow," he said in a warm and loving tone. "There is something I need to do, and I need you to trust me."

She pressed her face against his hand and looked into his eyes. "What is it?"

"I know you will object, but I need to go down there after my brother."

Her eyes widened and her face contorted. "Alone?"

"I'm afraid so. I won't let you risk your life on this. The team needs you now more than ever."

"But I want to help you!"

He held her tight and rested his chin on her shoulder. "Please, Sparrow, please trust me."

After giving her a tender kiss, he said, "I love you."

"I love you too," she whispered through grief-filled eyes.

Now pulling away, he got a running start and dove into the hole. Deeper and deeper he plummeted until the light from above vanished and cold darkness took its place.

18/NEXUS ORB

Hell is silence. The words echoed through James' mind as he fell further into the core of the planet. It was pitch black with nothing but the sound of air passing by to fill the empty void. He had been falling for over ten minutes and had not yet reached the bottom. A faint light was beginning to glow brighter the longer he descended, reminding him of the fact that the center of the planet was a molten ball of iron.

Kazav was picking up on James' fear. *"Relax, kid. If need be, I can wrap you in a protective cocoon that should keep the lava from incinerating you."*

"Good to know. By the way, what do we do even if we get to the Orb before Jeremy does?"

"Hmm, I'm not one hundred percent sure, but hiding it from the Guild might be a good idea."

Eventually, James reached a massive underground cave full of breathtaking crystals. He gasped as he looked on at the magical scene. Diamonds, rubies, emeralds, quartz, and almost every other gem imaginable lined the walls. Massive crystal columns grew and protruded out into the enormous hollow cave, some being the size of skyscrapers.

He sighed. "Incredible."

As quickly as they had entered, they left, continuing down the long tube to hell. It was starting to heat up as the light glowed brighter, and James braced for a magma bath. Oddly, the molten metal was pushed aside and suspended in the air as though something was keeping it at bay. They tumbled through the lava tunnel until it turned from bright yellow to a blinding white.

His fall slowed as he approached the center of the planet, and he entered a massive, hollow room. Lava was being held back by some unknown force, allowing him to pass through without the fear of being incinerated. There, in the center of the massive chamber, was a spherical ball rotating at a mind-boggling speed.

James' jaw dropped as he floated towards it. *"Could that be it?"*

Even Kazav sounded as though his breath had been stolen by the majesty. *"It's gotta be."*

James reached out to touch the polished surface of its perfectly sculpted casing but was blasted off to the side as Jeremy blocked him from getting any closer.

He wagged his finger as he teased them. "Ah, ah, ah. You didn't say the magic word."

James rubbed his shoulder and winced as a painful bruise formed where Jeremy had struck him. He held his ground rather than retaliate as he had no intention of fighting his brother, that was, if this person really was his brother.

"I'm surprised to see you down here, little bro. I didn't think you had the guts to follow after me."

"Cut the little bro talk, traitor."

"Okay, have it your way...little buddy. What's your plan with the Orb anyhow?" Jeremy asked out of genuine curiosity.

"To keep it as far away from you and the Guild as possible."

Jeremy moved in closer to the Orb, gripping its casing in his powerful hands. "I'm not sure what you think my intentions are. My only concern is protecting the Orb from people who would abuse it."

James moved around, trying to reverse their positions. "You say that, but everything you have said until now gives me plenty of reason to doubt you."

"What is there to doubt?" Jeremy asked with his arms outspread.

James looked at his brother, pain gripping his heart. He thought back to all the time they spent together before they grew apart. All the good times they shared, all the laughs, fights, and promises they made to one another. Promises like how they would never stop having each other's back, how they would never let each other down.

"Are you really my brother?"

Jeremy raised an eyebrow at the question. "What?"

"Are you really my brother?" he asked again, this

time shouting it.

Jeremy moved in closer as James spiraled. "Of course, I'm your brother," he replied in a genuine tone.

James looked into Jeremy's eyes. Tears floated out into the weightless chamber, turning into mist from the heat. "Then why did you abandon me?"

Jeremy froze in place, his face now shifting from angry to remorseful.

"Abandoned you?" he repeated softly. "I never abandoned you."

James turned his face away as he lost control of his emotions. "Maybe you never thought you did, but that's what it felt like to me. One day I had a brother I could count on, the next day I didn't. What word would you use to describe that?"

Jeremy thought back to the past. Back to all the times he left his brother to be bullied and harassed, all the times he ditched him to hang out with the other gifted kids, every moment he stole from James by instigating his parents into giving him more attention and praise.

Somehow, away from all the mindless diversions of the outside world, a tiny piece of humanity broke through. Maybe it was due to the proximity to the Orb, but Jeremy felt pain in his heart.

"Look, James, I'm not sure how you managed to get into this situation, nor do I understand the truth behind your strange new powers." He moved closer and put his hand on James' shoulder. A look of genuine concern and brotherly affection covered his eyes. It was an act of empathy James hadn't seen from his brother in a long time. "But if you are truly serious about protecting the Orb and are honestly looking out for the world, then maybe there's a way to meet in the middle. I can't promise that you'll be given everything you want, but I can promise to give you a voice."

He reached out his hand to shake. James looked down and then back up at his brother. With tears now flowing out he said, "It's a start...but I'll take it."

James' hand reached out for his brother's. He desperately wanted to mend things, and the shake would make it all feel official. The only problem was he could no longer move his own arms. He just floated there in midair, completely frozen as paralysis overwhelmed his body.

"Are you okay, brother?" Jeremy asked as he took hold of James' shoulder.

James' arm struck Jeremy and sent him flying out through the magma tube. The blow was so powerful it sent shockwaves through the chamber, creating swirling firestorms of raw iron.

"Kazav! What's happening? Why did you make me do that?"

"I'm sorry, kid. I can't let you give up. Not when we're this close."

From this point on, all of James' actions were involuntary as Kazav took control. He forced James to grab the casing the Nexus Orb was kept in and flew back up to the surface.

Jeremy crashed to the ground after regaining control and confronted his brother. "So that's the way you want it?" he shouted in guttural fury.

"No!" James cried out desperately. "I'm not doing this, I swear!"

"Enough! I'm going to put an end to this insanity."

He flew at James with all his might, sending out shockwaves that leveled everything in a mile radius. James winced in anticipation of the coming blow. He closed his eyes and prepared to face his end.

Jeremy's fist connected with his jaw and... nothing happened. While the power of his punch was enough to send ripples out through the city, shattering every window for miles, it seemed to have no effect on James. Another involuntary blow sent Jeremy flying out into the distance, giving Kazav time to peel apart the protective casing of the Nexus Orb.

James tried to fight back, but Kazav's control over him had become absolute. *"Kazav, what are you doing?"*

"What needs to be done, kid. I warned you about getting overly attached, and now this is the only way."

"Give me back control of my body!"

"I will. Just as soon as we're done here."

Now through the casing, Kazav forced James to reach in and take hold of the Orb. It was awe-inspiring to look at. A red, swirling sphere of untamed energy now lay in his hands, hypnotizing the eyes with its seductive allure.

Power surged through James in a way he had never felt before. It was like the entire universe was flowing through his mind. His body glowed like a star and sent waves of burning light streaking out in all directions. Buildings were sliced in half where the light made contact, and mountains were turned into heaps of rubble.

The last thing James experienced before passing out was the feeling of a million stars erupting in his soul and the sound of Kazav laughing like a madman.

19/BETRAYAL

James lay motionless on the ground. The muffled sounds of fighting and screaming lured him back to consciousness. It was hard for him to gauge just how long it had been since blacking out. A few minutes, days, weeks? An intense feeling kept pushing through the haze he was in, calling out for him to wake up. Reality rushed back, and he finally opened his eyes. Only, he opened them to a scene much different from the one they closed to.

Desolation was the only word he could think of to describe the city's state. Every skyscraper was leveled and almost nothing stood intact. The smell of melted metal and powdered concrete hung heavy in the air as fires burned out of control as far as the eye could see. At first, he was dazed and confused with little memory of what had happened. However, after looking over at the torn casing the Nexus Orb had been kept in, it all came rushing back.

With his fist and jaw clenched in a burning rage, he screamed out into the apocalyptic scene. "Kazav!"

There was no reply to his anger.

"Kazav!" he yelled once more. "I know you can hear me!"

It was then that James realized that for the first time in a while, Kazav wasn't there. He could no longer feel his presence within his mind or heart. Even the comically sadistic vibe he used to carry around in the back of his head was gone. He sat there, unsure of what to do, unsure of what to think.

He was hit with the realization that Sparrow and the rest of the team were still out there. What if they were trapped or in danger? He had to find them. He had to know they were okay.

As he stood up, he felt something he had not experienced in a long time. Dizziness. All the things that made him human took hold of him with a vengeance. Pain, nausea, a throbbing headache. Kazav used to control matters in such a way that James never felt anything other than powerful. Now that he was gone, James wondered if he even still retained his powers.

A small and puny stream of plasma flung from his hands as he tested his theory. It appeared he still had some minor abilities despite Kazav no longer residing within him. He staggered over the mounds of debris out into the city and made his way back to where the team had been stationed.

There was nothing in sight. Just a smoldering heap of half-vaporized brick and mortar from the local buildings that had been destroyed. With no sign of his team around, he headed back to the guildhall. He was holding out hope that they would be safe if the building stayed hidden by Sparrow's shadow abilities. Much to his horror, the entire building was not only visible, but completely decimated.

He called out for his friends, frantically shouting their names. "Sparrow! Static! Owl! Falcon! Hawk! Is anyone here? Can you hear me?" The only sound that could be heard in reply was the crackling of the fires that were burning the city to the ground.

He sank to the floor as dread gripped his heart. The thought of them being hurt, or worse, was too much for James to take. He broke down and a torrent of tears slid down his face and soaked the scorched ground below. For a moment the only sound to be heard was James' sobbing as he sat in the dirt, hoping against all odds his friends were still alive.

That was, until another noise echoed in the street. It was the unmistakable sound of boots clicking against the ground. They kept at a steady pace, clicking louder and louder with each step they took. Through the dust that hung in the air, a figure emerged. It looked human at first, its form kept obscured by the dust in the air.

The more focused the figure became, the more unusual its silhouette appeared. Jagged spikes and bony plates lined the being's body, and its limbs appeared gnarled and spindly. Oddly enough, as the being approached him, he felt a swell of power return, and his wound began to close shut. James looked on in silence as the mysterious being sauntered over. It stopped once it got within an arm's length and just stood there looking down at James in ambivalent silence.

Now that it was right in front of him, James could see every detail of its disgusting humanoid form. It was an odd mix of bone and sinew strung together like someone just slapped some rotting flesh on a skeleton. Pointed bones jutted out of its back and formed blades on each elbow. Its legs were a writhing mass of muscle and cartilage that went down until it met its feet, which were made of a solid, almost metallic material.

Even freakier was its face. A chiseled and armored plate of blood-red metal clung to the supple flesh that lay just below. Beady black eyes focused right on James and blinked, eyelids closing into a vertical slit.. The entire mask curled up into a bony crown fixed atop its head as if to imply he was king of some hideous nation.

They stayed like that for a time, James looking up at this odd creature while stuck in a state of emotional shock, the being staring back at him with a disturbing and expressionless face. Then, the being closed the gap and squatted beside him, its bones and flesh clacking and clicking together as it bent down. A mouth full of jagged, ebony teeth broke into a smile that was as wicked and vile as anything James could have imagined. It extended its wretched arm out and rested it on his shoulder. James wasn't afraid. He was too numb to feel fear.

"Hey, kid," the creature remarked, causing him to flinch.

James mouthed the words silently and connected the dots.

"Look, kid, before you get upset, let me exp-"

Kazav didn't have time to finish his sentence as James struck him in the face so hard it chipped off a piece of bone from his crown. Everything in front of the punch was shattered as the compressed air shunted everything out like hay blowing away in the wind.

"Fair enough," Kazav gurgled as he lay embedded in a slab of cement miles away.

Then, pulling his massive body out from the shattered foundation, he jetted back at James, leaving a trail of bright red energy in his wake. Soaring through the sky like a burning missile, he landed behind James, who was too slow to react. Grabbing him in his enormous hands, he lifted James off the ground and kept him at a distance. James tried kicking and punching Kazav like a child throwing a tantrum but couldn't reach his body.

"James!" Kazav shouted. "I know you're angry with me, and you have a right to be, but calm down!"

He wouldn't listen. Blind rage and agony overtook his heart and compelled him to do one thing and once thing only: kill Kazav.

"Liar!" James cried out as his fist met dead air.

"I'm not lying to you!"

Kazav saw that words would do no good. He looked on with pity at the sight before him. James was being held at arm's length like a cat being held by its scruff, tears streaming down his face as he shouted, "Die, you traitor! Die!"

Kazav let out a deep sigh as an odd tinge of guilt pricked his heart. He decided that since James wouldn't let him speak, he would just have to show him instead. Reaching out with his other hand, he grabbed James' head and fed him another vision.

With James now in a trance-like state, Kazav set him down on the ground to let him see the life-shattering experiences that led him to this moment. Why he lied, why he deceived James, why he stole the Nexus Orb, he wanted him to know everything.

James' eyes closed, and the memory began to play. He got to watch events unfold like a movie. Kazav's voice, the one he had when he was with James, narrated the scenes and added much-needed context and clarity.

The vision opened with a blue sun beaming light down on an unspoiled planet. Purple leaves dressed the exotic trees that covered the surface of the world, giving it an alien element. Children played in fields of wildflowers as their parents sprawled out on picnic baskets and enjoyed their lunch. Villas and villages dotted the landscape of this peaceful world in perfect balance with nature.

"Do you see the world below you, James? Do you see how pure and loving the people are? This is what I want for you, for the people of your planet."

The vision continued. Kazav traversed the planet, observing the creatures that called it home. He watched as lovers stole kisses in the night, as people grieved at their lost loved ones, and observed all the little moments that made up their short, intense lives.

"It was all so fascinating to me, watching as they grew older each day. How they smiled when they ate, laughed as they danced, and cried when they got injured. There was something so...incredible about their fragility. I wanted to know what it was like. I too wanted to feel what they felt every waking moment."

Now scenes of Kazav interacting with a particular villager flew by. James saw their first interactions together. The man freaked out when first hearing Kazav's voice, but in time, they appeared to grow into close friends.

"His name was Felton, and he was the kindest man I had ever known. I knew from the beginning that he was the person I wanted to bond with. It would be through his eyes that I experienced the world. With Felton, I experienced the thrills of a first kiss, the joys of fatherhood, and the pain of losing a spouse. Do you know what it taught me, James? It taught me that life is precious. I hope you can see that."

More time passed, and James watched as Felton grew older and older. Now approaching the end of his life, he watched as the man took his last breath, slowly loosening his grip around his child's hand. Kazav stuck by his side to the very end but was forced back to his home world once the bond was broken. He was imprisoned by the judges of his world and forced to lay shackled to the ground for a thousand years.

"Do you know what kept me going the entire time I was restrained? It was the thought of returning to that beautiful world. To go back and form new bonds, new friendships, and to make life the best it could be for those fragile mortal beings."

Once released from his bonds, Kazav made his way back to the planet only to find it in shambles. In the thousand years that passed, war and disease killed off millions of innocents. Crime and violence turned the once-peaceful world into a cesspool of pain and agony. Through all his attempts to turn things around, Kazav was met with resistance until eventually, the planet turned into a lifeless rock.

"Do you see what they did to themselves? Without the right guidance, they turned their home into a wasteland. The same thing is happening to your world, James. That's why I have come here. To put an end to this insanity. I won't let what happened to them happen to you as well."

Now flying through space, Kazav landed on a familiar planet. It was James' home. James watched as Kazav spent months observing the people go about their daily lives. Millions of faces flipped by until it came to rest on his own.

"I spent a lot of time trying to find you, James. Just like Felton, there was something special inside you, something so few people possess. You were willing to die for the good of others, to throw your self-interest by the wayside and promote the greater good.

That's why I chose you, why I wanted to bond with you."

Continuing the vision, Kazav showed James events during their time together. It was all from Kazav's perspective. He watched as he steered James in a certain direction during key moments, how he influenced him into making choices he never would have made on his own, and how he used lies to get James to believe what he wanted him to believe. James even watched as Kazav revealed how he started the Cleansers for his own benefit, how he used them to manipulate the world and distract them from realizing his real goal.

The vision faded until James was staring out into a black void.

"So, you see, James, I couldn't let you fail. I couldn't let *us* fail. All the lies, all the trickery, it was all for the greater good. I hope you can understand that."

"Why couldn't you have just been honest? Why did you have to lie to me?"

"Something I came to understand about humans while I sifted through the millions in my search for someone like you was this: humans are selfish. They would never willingly submit to being ruled even if it was for their own benefit. That was the mistake I made in my first attempt. No matter how much pain they inflicted on themselves, they resisted my attempts to save them. Eventually, it led to their own extinction."

"But why steal the Nexus Orb? Why turn into

this...thing?"

Kazav let out a sigh. He was genuinely pained at the hurt James was feeling. But like tearing off a Band-Aid, Kazav was not about to let his emotions cloud the bigger issue.

"The Nexus Orb was necessary for a few reasons. The first was eliminating all threats to my rule. With the Orb's power drained, the heroes of your world lose their powers. The second reason I sought the Orb is to have a body of my own. So immense is the Orb's energy that it alone contained the power I need to seal my quantum essence in a physical form. Had I tried to stay in your body, you would have eventually taken back control. I'm so sorry about all this, kid, I truly am. I just couldn't let another planet die off because of its inhabitants' stupidity. It's just too...painful to watch."

James remained silent for a long time. The scenes from Kazav's vision were still racing through his mind. It was so confusing, deciding how to feel. On one hand, James had seething anger boiling in his heart, but on the other hand, he could truly understand all that Kazav had been through. James knew his planet was killing itself just as Kazav claimed. Pollution, war, crime – they were running amok with no end in sight. But was this really the way to solve it? Was domination of a species through malicious force ever going to be the solution? James was at a loss for words.

"Kazav, I don't...know what to say. I'm so confused."

"I know, kid, I know. You don't need to understand everything. All you need to know is I'm here to help. With my guidance, I will turn your world into the pure, pain-free environment you always dreamed of. All you need to do is trust me."

He began to consider what Kazav was saying. What if this was the best way forward? Kazav had the power to change things for the better – wasn't that what he wanted all along? Then he started thinking about Sparrow, about what she would do. Sparrow stood against the concept of using evil to an end. No matter how noble the intention, she refused to justify the wicked means. She wouldn't side with Kazav. She would stand against him.

"Well, kid, what's it going to be? Will you join me in reshaping this corrupt world into one of peace? Or are you going to throw away your life based on some misguided sense of justice? It's time for you to choose."

James was now back in the awful reality Kazav had created. The city, and everything in it, had been leveled and scorched. All the heroes that could have stood against him lay motionless on the ground, rendered powerless without the Orb's energy.

"What's it going to be?" Kazav repeated to James. "Life or death?"

James was torn. He did want to change the world. He did want to get rid of all the horrible elements that were dragging it down into oblivion, but he wondered if this was the way to do it. What about all the people who would resist? James knew full well that humans were stubborn and proud. He knew they wouldn't just sit down and accept being dominated even if it was for their own good.

And then there was Sparrow. He knew exactly what she would do in this situation. She was always so headstrong and confident. It was a quality of hers he often envied. In the end, James sided with the one person who had never steered him wrong, the one person who he knew he could trust to the very end.

Kazav could sense what James was thinking. "Don't let your emotions color your judgment, kid. I did that one too many times, and it always leads to pain."

"What if I take your side? What happens then?" James asked while looking into Kazav's beady, black eyes.

"Then you get to join me in reshaping this world and snuffing out every last self-destructive person in existence."

James thought about what he was saying. That would mean the slaughter of millions, if not billions of people.

"And if I take the opposing side?"

Kazav's face curled into a frown. The very fact that James would ask that left a bitter taste in his mouth. "Then I will have no choice but to dispose of you along with any other person who stands in the way of harmony."

"I see."

As James lay on the ground, thoughts racing through his mind, a smile grew on his face. He realized that all this time, Kazav might have been trying to influence him to do his bidding, but in the end, Sparrow was the one who had the greatest impact on him. The choice was now clear. He wanted to be like her and choose the right path, the path that few else would choose. He was going to be a real hero, the hero he always dreamed of being.

He stood up and took a defensive stance. "I'm sorry, my old friend, but I can't. I can't betray the people of this world. Despite all you have endured, I just won't do it. I'm sorry."

Kazav let out a disappointed sigh. "That's upsetting, kid, but I understand."

With that, he grabbed James and held him up above his head, squeezing his body with immense force. He opened his disfigured maw like a snake unhinging its jaw. Moments later, a red light glowed in the back of his throat, humming as he charged a deadly attack.

"It didn't have to be this way, James. I take no joy in doing this."

James tried to squirm out of his grasp, but he couldn't. All he could do was watch as an eruption of searing hot energy blasted out of Kazav's mouth and struck James head-on. He cried out as the stream of power engulfed his body and started turning his skin red from the heat.

Kazav grew puzzled. He didn't understand how James was still able to resist such a devastating strike. Now that he was out of James' body and no longer offering direct aid, that beam should've turned him to dust. He decided to turn up the heat, making the beam wider and stronger. James' skin turned white-hot from the heat and was burning Kazav's hand. He shut off the beam and tried another approach.

"If that won't do the job, then maybe this will."

Kazav's hideous and bulging muscles tightened and flexed as he clamped his hands around James and squeezed with all his might. With pressure that could make a diamond from coal, James grunted and groaned as he was held aloft and pressed tight by Kazav's wretched, bony fingers.

The harder Kazav tried to squash him, the less of an effect it seemed to have.

"This makes no sense," he cried out as James hacked and coughed on the floor.

"Unless..." Kazav mumbled as he stroked his metallic chin. "Unless our bond can only truly break when you die. That would mean that while we were still physically paired, everything that happened to me would also happen to you."

James laughed as he stood back up. "Which means that when you received the Nexus Orb's power, so did I. Now that I think about it, the closer I get to you, the more powerful I feel. Why might that be?"

Now just an arm's length away from Kazav, James decided it was his turn to offer a choice. "Seeing as how I still hold the power to stop you, I'll give you two options. The first is you give your power back to the Orb and leave this planet forever."

Kazav gave a sinister snicker. He was both intimidated and entertained by James' threatening demeanor. "And the second choice?" Kazav asked with an intrigued smile.

James raised his fist and said, "The second choice is I beat it out of you."

Now with a full-on manic laugh, Kazav stood up to his full height and towered over James. He brought his head down and looked him in the eyes.

"In that case..." He paused for dramatic effect. "Good luck."

No sooner did he finish his sentence did James get sent flying backward as Kazav came at him with full force. Every strike, every hit, every move was now at a level so powerful that shockwaves raced out in all directions, flattening any building still left standing. Beams of energy shot out from Kazav's jaws, darting toward James, who dodged and weaved between them.

Kazav's assault was relentless, and James was doing everything he could just to not get pummeled. Every hit that connected sent them smashing into the ground, throwing massive heaps of stone flying into the sky. James' main concern was getting Kazav away from the city. He wanted to keep collateral damage to a minimum.

Now hundreds of miles away from anything, James fought back with incredible power. His hits, even when held back, would turn everything in front of him to dust. The power of his blows was so immense that it blasted holes in mountains, rerouted rivers, and flattened forests.

After hours of fighting, the gouges in the ground became so deep that magma filtered through the cracks. James worried that their fight was putting the planet in jeopardy, and he turned away for a fraction of a second to survey the damage. Kazav took advantage of his momentary preoccupation and landed an uppercut on him so forceful that it shot him into the atmosphere.

A flashing streak of light flooded his eyes, rendering him momentarily blind. Once his senses returned, his jaw dropped as he realized he was being held aloft, floating in place as he looked back on the planet from above.

James was overtaken by its beauty. The crystal blue ocean, the teeming forests that painted the landmasses green – it was all so magical. Looking up, he could see the northern lights dancing high above in the atmosphere. Then, looking down, he could see the ice shelves that dominated the southern pole.

As quickly as he was sent up, he was sent back down by yet another surprise strike from Kazav. Like an asteroid streaking through the sky, James crashed into the planet's surface, smashing into the ground with the force of an atomic bomb.

With his focus back on Kazav, James really let loose. Massive streams of black plasma flowed out from his hands as he attempted to vaporize the alien. The world around them morphed into an ocean of bubbling liquid rock as they fired stream after stream of energy attacks at one another. After several more hours of planet-shattering, rock-melting, and bone-crushing combat, they began to lose steam and, while taking a brief respite, stood across from each other, their eyes locked in a hateful gaze.

"Had enough?" James mocked.

"I could do this all day!" Kazav quipped. While staring one another down, Kazav decided to offer an olive branch. "Look, kid, out of respect for you and all we went through, I'm willing to give you one last chance to be on the right side of history."

James shook his head vigorously. "No chance, Kazav, no chance at all."

"Well then, it looks like I need to bring this game to its end."

Kazav let loose a flurry of blows that sent James racing through the sky. There was no time to dodge, no time to deflect; he was teaching James the hard way that he had been holding back.

With James now lodged into the side of a mountain, Kazav rallied every bit of energy he could. Like a star in the night sky, he glowed as a vortex of red and purple energy swirled around him, bathing him in a wicked energy. Finally, he unleashed a beam on James that was so powerful it turned everything within a hundred-mile radius into a burning heap of molten slag.

Kazav scanned the area to ensure that James had not managed to escape. Convinced the only threat to his reign was gone, he returned to the city to finish what he started.

20/POWERLESS

Sparrow rubbed her head as she emerged from the rubble. The last thing she remembered was fighting off an influx of monsters that had overrun the sector. Tears filled her eyes as she looked upon the city. Fires burned, choking the air in black soot.

The sounds of people moving through the rubble grew into a grim chorus of moans and groans. Hawk and Falcon were digging themselves out from a pile of loose brick while Owl clambered up from a ditch. Static winced in pain as she crawled out from under a partially collapsed wall.

Sparrow noticed something odd – they were all covered in wounds. She had never seen so many little cuts and bruises on them before. Sure, they got injured during fights, but this was different.

"What happened?" Static called out.

Sparrow threw a few stones off from the pile she sat in. "I have no idea."

"Ahhh!" Falcon cried out in pain as he fell to the ground.

"What? What is it?" Sparrow asked.

"My foot!" he moaned while pointing down at

the jagged piece of rebar protruding from his foot.

"Lay him down over here," Sparrow commanded, pointing to a mattress that lay in the middle of the street.

They carried him over to the mattress, cleaned off the rubble, and gently set him down.

Sparrow was confused. The team didn't get injured from things as minor as all this. They could fly through buildings without a single scratch! Why was it suddenly so different?

Owl gripped the rebar pole and casually remarked, "I apologize for what I'm about to do next."

Falcon then let out a blood-curdling scream as Owl yanked it out of his foot. They bandaged it and addressed their own wounds. Everyone then looked up at the sky as a fireball streaked across the horizon, landing close to where their guildhall was stationed.

Sparrow had a bad feeling growing in her gut. Something was very wrong, and she needed to find out what. "Everyone, stay here and take care of Falcon. I will be right back."

Hawk grabbed her arm, forcing her to turn and face him. "Where are you going?"

Sparrow ordered him to let go. "I'm going to check something out. I won't be gone long. Just stay here and keep each other safe!"

Static ran over and grabbed her by the hand. "I'm not letting you go out there alone."

Sparrow shook her off and commanded, "I'm

not asking, I'm telling you. I promise I will be right back. Just stay here and keep out of sight!"

They watched as she sprinted away from them out into the ruined city.

"Should we go after her?" Static asked.

Hawk shook his head. "No, she's our guild master, and she gave us an order. Our duty is to follow those orders. Now then, Owl, Static, help me move Falcon to a more secure location."

Now running through the ruins of the city she loved, Sparrow wheezed and panted. No longer could she leap and bound over cars and buildings like before. Now she was confined to a slow, lazy stagger.

Upon reaching the guildhall, she fell to her knees. Looking on at the heap it had been reduced to, she cried bitter, bitter tears.

Her sobs were interrupted by the sound of something pushing through the rubble. It sounded like someone was underneath the remains of the hall, trying desperately to escape."

"Hello? Is someone there? Can you hear me?"

Piles of stone and wood erupted into the air, sending massive slaps crashing back down into the field around her. She leaped to the side, narrowly avoided being crushed by a foundation block.

Hovering above her head was a figure she couldn't make out. It was obscured by the dust hanging heavy in the air.

"James! Is that you? Oh, please let it be you!"

"James?" the figure repeated in a wicked tone. "I suppose you could say I am a little bit James."

Sparrow backed away as a horrifying creature approached her, its metallic boots clicking against the ground with every step.

Now directly in front of her, it let out a greeting. "Hello, Sparrow," the creature remarked as it bared rows of razor-sharp teeth through a wretched smile.

Her eyes narrowed. "How do you know my name?"

"Oh, I know a lot about you, little lady. Let's just say I have gotten to know you quite well over the past year."

She was lost. Why was this ugly creature talking to her in such a familiar tone?

"Who, or *what* are you?" she asked as it flexed its bony spine.

"Where are my manners? My name is Kazav, and I am here to make your life much, much better than you could have ever hoped!"

"Make my life better? What do you mean?"

Kazav bent down to her level, much like an adult kneeling when speaking to a child.

"I know firsthand how much you hate the lying and corrupt figures of this world, Sparrow. You haven't realized this yet, but you and I have been friends for a while."

She looked at him with disgust. "I have never

seen you before in my entire life."

Kazav chuckled. "You're right. You haven't seen me before, but *I* have seen *you*."

"What? What are you talking about? Explain yourself right now, you freaky bone guy!"

"I would, but I doubt you would believe me."

She crossed her arms. "Try me."

Kazav shrugged. "All right, don't say I didn't warn you."

He sat down on a chunk of rubble and began his explanation. "James and I were bonded together in a quantum relationship. Think of it as the kind of relationship some fungi have with trees, only much more complex."

Sparrow's face lit up. "You know James?"

"Oh, yeah, I knew him. Matter of fact, he and I are the whole reason all of this happened!"

She moved closer. "What do you mean, you guys are the reason all this happened? And why are you speaking in the past tense?"

Kazav sighed. "I hate to be the one to tell you this, but James is no longer with us."

Sparrow's heart sank. "What? What are you talking about?

Kazav just sat there unsure of what else to say.

"Answer me!" Sparrow commanded.

"I'm sorry to say that James did not want to take part in the paradise I was going to make for all of you.

He chose to stand in the way of progress, so I had to... eliminate him."

Sparrow flew into a rage. "I don't know who you are or what you are talking about, but if you lay even one bony finger on James, I'll kill you!"

Kazav stood back up and wagged his finger. "Little lady, I would advise you to calm down. If you try to attack me, it won't go down how you think it will."

Sparrow ran at him, attempting to form a shadow knife. A weak, blinking blade formed for a moment and then vanished. She tried again and again but couldn't keep it from sputtering out.

"See," Kazav mocked. "I told you so."

She ran at him regardless, letting out a scream as she tried to kick and punch through his armored body. Her knuckles soon became bloody and torn as her blows did nothing but serve as a minor nuisance.

"Where is James?" she screamed. "What did you do?"

"I just told you what I did. He is gone, dead, sleeping forever – there are only so many ways I can phrase it, toots."

"Liar! You're lying!" she shouted with blood and tears flowing in equal measure.

"Afraid not, hon. Now unlike him, you still have the option of living in a great new world with me as your king! I would make sure nothing ever hurt you again. Wouldn't you like that?"

"Get away from me!" she screamed. "You're not a

king of anything, and I wouldn't listen to you even if you were!"

"Oh," Kazav mumbled. "So, you too, huh?"

His body language changed from friendly to threatening. "I really didn't want it to be this way, Sparrow. I had truly come to care for you just like I cared for James, but I won't let this world die like the others. I just won't."

He opened his massive jaws and started charging an energy beam. Tripping as she moved back, Sparrow tried to crawl away. Pinning her to the ground, Kazav aimed at her head, eager to end things as quickly as possible

"Just hold still, and I promise you won't feel a thing."

She tried to jerk her foot free, but she was trapped. As the laser built in his mouth, Sparrow closed her eyes and accepted her fate.

Instead of being vaporized, Kazav dropped her as he was sent flying by a massive stream of glowing plasma. There, standing at the top of a hill, was James, smoke exuding off him. Sparrow ran over with her hands outstretched.

"I'm so glad you're okay!" she cried out. Her joy then mixed with fear as she looked over his scorched body. "What happened to you?

He pulled her close and hugged her, running his fingers through her hair as she gripped him tight. "It's okay, Sparrow, I'm fine."

A sonic boom in the distance served as a warning that Kazav was on his way back, cutting their reunion short.

"Sparrow, listen very carefully. I need you to join the rest of the team and find someplace safe to hide until this is over. Do you understand?"

She objected, gripping him tighter and refusing to let go. "Please, I don't want to leave you again."

"I know, but I need you to trust me."

She hesitated at first, but then conceded. "Okay, I trust you."

James smiled and gave her a wink. "Good, now go as fast as you can!"

She took off running while James stood poised to meet Kazav and finish this once and for all.

"You are a lot more durable than I thought!" Kazav complimented as he touched down in front of James.

"Sorry to disappoint."

"No biggie! Just stand still, and I will make sure to end your pain as quickly as possible."

"You know, when you first betrayed me, I was willing to let you go provided you never show your face on this planet again. I would have still extended that courtesy to you now had you not done the one thing I could never forgive."

Kazav raised an eyebrow, his curiosity now piqued. "And what might that be?"

James launched forward in the blink of an eye and took him by surprise. Then, as they were face to face, he said in a deadly soft voice, "You tried to hurt my Sparrow."

A blast of plasma erupted from James' hand and enveloped Kazav, hurling him against the ground and coating him in corrosive gel. He was quick to shake it off, but James was already on top of him, landing blow after blow against his ever-weakening armor.

Kazav tried to shield himself, but the blows were so fierce it made little difference. Rather than defend, he shot out into the sky, taking James along with him. They flew across the land and wrestled in midair as each tried to get the advantage over the other.

"It's impolite to grab people!" Kazav shouted as James held onto him by one of his bone ridges.

"It's also impolite to be this ugly!"

With a swift strike from his elbow, he sent Kazav crashing down to the ground along with several of his protective plates. Streams of bright light peeked out from behind the damaged sections of Kazav's armor, giving James a sudden realization.

Once more, a powerful burst of energy shot out from Kazav's mouth only for it to be stopped in midair by James. Twirling the beam around, he absorbed its energy until it vanished inside his body.

Kazav was shocked. "What did you just do?"

"Oh, that? I just absorbed your laser, so, no biggie. Oh, and look what I can make it do!"

James pointed his finger at Kazav and returned the laser back at him. Kazav tried to dodge it, but it clipped his shoulder and sent another piece of his plating flying off.

He rubbed his shoulder and winced. "So that's how you survived? By absorbing the beam?"

James shook his head. "Deflected is more like it. After taking it head-on for a bit, I started to get the feel for it, to understand it better. It seems like the more you use your power against me, the better I get at manipulating it."

Kazav clapped. "I must admit, I'm impressed. I suppose I shouldn't be, but I am." His clapping then slowed until it came to a complete stop. "But now I need to end this so I can get to work. So, if you don't mind, I need you to die now."

Kazav shot forward with his hands outstretched, eager to end the battle. James stood there motionless as if he wasn't going to offer any resistance. He closed his eyes as Kazav approached and took a deep breath in and out.

"That's the idea, kid, just hold still, and I'll make it as painless as possible."

He flung his arm forward at James but came to a standstill just before he could close his grip.

Kazav looked down at his motionless body. "What's happening? What did you do?"

James opened his eyes, a massive grin growing on his face. "I realized something about our relationship, Kazav."

Kazav let out a laugh. "And what is it you learned, pray tell?"

While walking around Kazav's motionless form, James explained, "Remember when you took control of me and forced me to attack Jeremy and steal the Nexus Orb?"

Kazav was growing concerned. He didn't like where this was going.

"Well, my freaky friend, it was while you were blasting me with laser beams that I began to theorize if that ability was a two-way street. Now that you have a body, I wondered if I too could control you like you controlled me."

Now Kazav was worried. If what James was saying was true, then he might have made a huge mistake. But in no time, concern was replaced by a devious grin. "You're right, kid, it is a two-way street."

James jerked and twitched as Kazav tried to bring his body under control. A tug of war was now taking place as each of them invaded the other's mind, attempting to subdue them.

Kazav was trying to exert a strong influence, but now that he was no longer inside James, he found it difficult to override his willpower. The battle pointed at a clear winner as James shunted off Kazav's attempts and sent out a wave of raw, irresistible resolve that brought Kazav completely under his command.

"Why is this so difficult?" Kazav cried out in frustration.

James forced him to kneel so he could talk face to face. "I have had a body my entire life. You have only had one for less than a day. Do you know how much willpower it takes to be a human, Kazav? How much strength it takes to get up every day and decide to keep going? Do you have any clue what it takes to endure the heartbreak of losing love? Of losing a mother, a father, or even your best friend?"

Kazav grew sullen, his hideous features drooping as memories of all the people he used to love came flooding back. All the pain they felt, all the loss they endured. He wished he could have truly understood what it was like, but at best he was just an observer.

"That's why I did all this, James. I wanted to end that feeling, to make it so you never felt anything but joy and contentment. Sure, it would take some sacrifice, but wouldn't it be worth it?"

James nodded. "Kazav, it won't work. Even if you brought about peace for a while, it wouldn't last. I won't be party to mass murder even if it's based on good intentions."

The sullen look was replaced with anger as Kazav yelled, "Then you, along with everyone who dares to keep this dying world alive, will be annihilated!"

James opened his hand as if to hold something. A shimmering plasma blade formed, and he gripped it tight.

Kazav tried to move, but his body was locked. He was, however, still able to spit out lasers, and he sent out shot after shot.

James deflected them with his sword and, using a hand motion, forced Kazav's mouth shut. Then, bringing the blade up, he plunged it deep into Kazav's chest, causing a stream of glowing red light to flow out of his body and swirl around like crimson snow.

Kazav let out muffled screams of pain from the intense burning roiling through his body. James forced the blade in further and mercilessly carved out a massive molten hole.

The stream of red energy was now pouring out like a river, forming into a sphere in the air above them. James retracted the blade and backed away from the creature now writhing on the ground in agony.

Hunks of rancid meat plopped onto the ground as Kazav's body fell apart. The bony plating that protected his innards disassembled and turned to dust.

For a moment, Kazav had a strange look on his face. It was neither remorse nor sorrow, not anger or rage. James could only wonder what Kazav's final thoughts were as he erupted in a fiery explosion, sending bone shards and cooked flesh in every direction.

A tear streaked down James' face, mixed emotions tugging at him. "Goodbye, my old friend."

Still swirling overhead, James channeled the energy released from Kazav into a sphere, gripping it firmly in his hands. Sparrow had been watching all along and ran out to be by his side. In her excitement, she jumped out to hug him, almost tackling him to the ground.

"I'm so glad you're okay!" she cried out.

"Me too, Sparrow," he replied softly.

She looked over at the glowing red ball he was holding. "What's that?"

James held it up. "This is part of the Nexus Orb."

"Incredible!" she exclaimed. "So that monster tried to steal it? That would explain why everyone lost their powers," she remarked while looking at her hands.

James asked her if she knew how to return the Orb to its original state.

"No idea."

"I know how," a voice shouted from behind.

They turned to see Jeremy swaying as he walked through the torn-up landscape. Sparrow got in a defensive position and warned him not to try anything.

"You know how to fix the Orb and give the heroes their power back?" James asked.

Jeremy nodded. "The Orb is not unlimited in its power, but it can regenerate. That's why it was housed in the planet's core. In there it can utilize the planet's rotational energy and provide a limitless supply of power to every hero in the world."

"Wait," Sparrow interrupted, "you're saying that the Orb has to be put back in the planet's core?

"That is correct."

"There is no way you are going back down there!" she chided James. "It's way too dangerous!"

James tenderly caressed her cheek with his hand and brought her eyes to his. "The Orb will keep me safe until I put it back in the core. Then, once it's in place, I will just head to the surface, and everything will be fine."

"No!" she shouted. "There has to be a better way!"

"I'm the only one who can do this, Sparrow. No other hero has their abilities besides me."

She started to object but was unable to refute the argument. "Just...please come back safe. I love you."

James kissed her and replied, "I love you too."

With that, he flew off into the sky, heading for the hole Jeremy had previously blasted into the ground. He reached the tube and hurtled down as fast as he could. Tears flew off his face and out into the air as he descended.

The truth was he had no idea if he was coming back. Once the Orb was back in place, he would need to return the energy residing in his body. In addition, with the Orb no longer holding back the magma, he would need to pass through it, billions of tons separating him from his goal. The tube glowed red-hot and in no time, he reached the fluid-like mantel. With no hesitation, he dove straight in and swam toward the core. It was hot, so very hot, but he kept pushing. His hair burned off the deeper into the magma he sank. Pressure built to almost unbearable levels as the weight of the planet was now pushing on him in all directions.

Eventually, he reached the core. The thick swirling ball of liquid iron stood in sharp contrast with the molten rock surrounding it. Wading through the viscus metal, he headed deeper still and held out his hand, releasing the power of the Orb.

It floated out of its own volition and took its place back in the very center of the planet. He expected some grand display now that it had returned, but nothing happened. The glowing red ball just floated there in the middle of the burning ocean.

James then remembered he would need to return the energy still contained within his own body, so he moved in closer and held out his arms. Once the ball rested back in his hands, he gave it all the juice he had left.

His life played out before him from the start of it up to this moment. A deep, ponderous nostalgia grew in his heart as the entirety of his existence was laid bare. It felt like comfort, like bliss, like how a child felt when it was safe in its mother's arms.

Despite being surrounded by liquid rock, he grew colder. His limbs tingled and lost their feeling. As the last remaining ounces of the Orb's power drained out from his body, the cascade of mental images slowed until it came to a stop. With the power of the Orb now fully restored, it rotated just like before, and heroes around the world cried out with joy as their powers returned.

James drifted out into the sea of magma, a smile adorning his face.

With his final thought being of Sparrow's warm, loving embrace, James closed his eyes and surrendered to the darkness.

Made in United States
North Haven, CT
05 June 2022

19859737R00146